The English Garden Mystery

A Problem in Deduction

ALSO BY DAN ANDRIACCO

The Sebastian McCabe—Jeff Cody Mysteries
No Police Like Holmes
Holmes Sweet Holmes
The 1895 Murder
The Disappearance of Mr. James Phillimore
Rogues Gallery
Bookmarked for Murder
Erin Go Bloody
Queen City Corpse
Death Masque
Too Many Clues
Murderers' Row
No Ghosts Need Apply

The Enoch Hale Trilogy (with Kieran McMullan)
The Amateur Executioner
The Poisoned Penman
The Egyptian Curse

Sherlock Holmes
Baker Street Beat
House of the Doomed
The Sword of Death

School for Sleuths
School for Sleuths
The Medium is the Murder

The English Garden Mystery

A Problem in Deduction

Dan Andriacco

Paperback ISBN 978-1-80424-081-6
ePub ISBN 978-1-80424-082-3
PDF ISBN 978-1-80424-083-0

Published by MX Publishing
335 Princess Park Manor, Royal Drive,
London, N11 3GX
www.mxpublishing.com
Cover design by Brian Belanger

This book is in memory of
Frederic Dannay
and Manfred B. Lee
(Ellery Queen)

CONTENTS

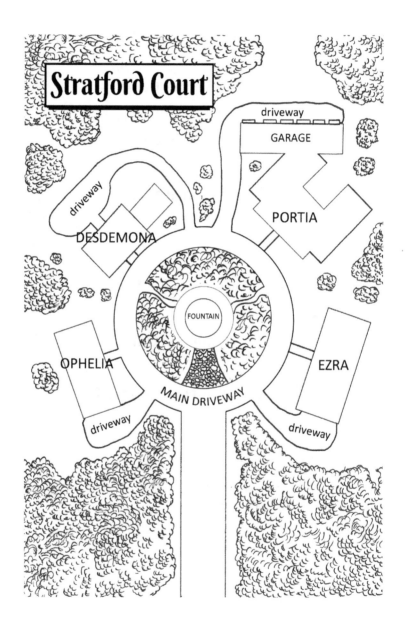

Chapter One
A Summer's Day

This story begins in a garden. But so does the third chapter of Genesis, as Sebastian McCabe reminded me recently, and that one had a snake in it.

The lovely English garden of which I write, maintained almost full time by a not-so-English gardener, is at the center of the Bainbridge family compound of houses collectively known as Stratford Court. It's a riot of roses, daffodils, marigolds, daisies, and more exotic plants with an ornate bronze fountain in the shape of a flute-playing Pan at the center.

And on the 31st of July in the second year of the worldwide COVID-19 pandemic, it seemed like half our little town of Erin, Ohio, was assembled there under a clear-blue sky to party to the music of a string trio and the flowing of champagne. I didn't see much evidence of what one psychiatrist called "cave syndrome," the fear of going out in society months after vaccination was widespread. Nor had the Delta variant caused widespread re-masking in our corner of the universe. (Omicron was just a little-known letter of the Greek alphabet at the time.) What I did see a lot of was badly executed do-it-yourself haircuts.

"Des Bainbridge has to be thrilled with this turnout," I commented to Lynda between sips of domestic bubbly from Erin's own Silk Stocking winery. Des was the hostess of this fund-raiser for the Erin Arts Council, which was sponsoring a new artist-in-residence program at the Shinkle Museum of Art. Everybody important in town had turned out for it, including Mayor Fred Sutterlee and our politically ambitious county prosecutor, Marvin Slade.

"The timing was right for any event that's not virtual," Lynda observed. "Even though things have been opening up for a few months now, we're all still stir-crazy from a year of social distancing and Zoom meetings. Look at Portia." That was no unpleasant task. Portia Bainbridge, in her early forties, was a tall blonde with chin-length hair, blue-eyed and attractive, just like her sisters Desdemona and Ophelia—no surprise, given that they were triplets; not identical, which is extremely rare, but close enough to fool me. As the father of almost-four-year-old twin boys and their older sister, I couldn't imagine the task of rearing three the same age. Especially since their mother, Juliet Bainbridge, died at their birth. "She's wobbling on her feet in those Vince Camuto pumps with the four-inch heels," Lynda added. "She's still out of practice."

Portia did walk a little like a baby giraffe as she clumsily worked the crowd, moving from Dr. Trixie LaBelle, my urologist, to Dr. Dante Peter O'Neill, Dean of St. Benignus University's Rev. Joseph F. Pirelli School of Arts and Humanities. Although she was the most socially conscious of the sisters Bainbridge, and former president of the Junior League of Erin, she was also the one most attached to the garden. From what Fred Gaffe told me one night at Bobbie McGee's Sports Bar before his untimely demise,[1]

---

[1] See *No Ghosts Need Apply*, MX Publishing, 2021.

Portia spent a lot of time with the gardener. That stuck in my mind because I thought she only talked to flowers and rich people. Her husband busied himself with his car collection and risky investments, according to the Old Gaffer.

My comely spouse, in contrast to Portia, wore glittery sandals that showed off her pretty feet with toenails painted green and pink to look like watermelons. She'd opted for a sporty look with a straw trilby hat over her dark-honey curls, sunglasses, and a short yellow off-the-shoulder sundress that hugged her bounteous bosom. The intoxicating smell of her Cleopatra VII perfume wafted my way on a gentle breeze as I watched Ezra Bainbridge roll by in a wheelchair pushed by his much-younger wife, Fleur. Never a tall man, the *pater familias* of one of the oldest of Erin's old-money families had shrunken over the past year. He'd also developed mobility problems that made moving on wheels easier for him, although I'd also seen him use a cane.

"He does not look well, does he?" came a rumble in my left ear.

Not unless you like the death-warmed-over effect.

"You must be a detective," I quipped to my corpulent brother-in-law, whose successes as an amateur sleuth are the subject of these chronicles. "I hope his will is up to date."

Sebastian McCabe, decked out in a linen suit and carrying his walking stick with the top carved in the shape of a hound's head, ignored the Cody sarcasm, as is his habit. "Kate tells me that he is battling brain fog in the wake of COVID-19, old boy."

Kathleen Cody McCabe, my sister, who was chatting at the other end of the garden with the Shinkle's Adam Mendenhall, occasionally lunched with Des Bainbridge to talk about arty matters. Her intel about the state of Ezra's health was of some professional interest to me because Ezra was on the board of trustees of St. Benignus, where I labor as vice president of marketing and communications (a new title with no raise attached) and Mac is a professor of English and director of the tiny popular culture program. The third Bainbridge sister, Ophelia, was also an SBU English prof with one foot in Mac's popular culture sandbox.

"I'm sorry to hear that," I said. "That's tough."

"It's been a tough year," Lynda put in. "Everything's changed."

The proof of that was right in front of me as I looked around. Handshaking, hugs, and social kisses—while by no means absent—were in relatively limited supply on this beautiful summer's day. Lynda's journalistic protégé, Johanna Rawls of *The Erin Observer & News-Ledger*, stood several feet away from Serena Mason as they talked animatedly. Partying wasn't as hearty as it would have been two years before (although Tall Rawls, a six-footer even taller in heels, and her much-shorter boyfriend, Seth Miller, weren't keeping any social distance).

Johanna and Serena stopped in mid-kvetch as Frank Woodford, editor and general manager of the *Observer*, walked by them on his way to our trio a few yards away. That made me wonder what they'd been talking about.

Frank bowed toward Lynda, who had worked either for him or with him for years as a journalist before going freelance, then turned his attention to Mac and me. In his late sixties, two decades older than me, his remaining hair was no longer as black as his face but now mostly white.

"So, how are things going in the groves of academe, gentlemen?" he asked.

"A-Plus," I said.

"The students will be back soon," Mac reported, almost sounding as if that were a good thing. Maybe he was thinking of the local restaurants, bars, shops, and hotels that were seeing their businesses rise from the dead as our young scholars moved back in with parental help. "However, the pandemic has posed quite an economic challenge to the university. Jefferson could tell you more about that."

Not if I can help it.

I changed the subject, telling Frank: "I bet you know everybody here."

"Pretty much everybody," he admitted. "That's my job."

He exaggerated only slightly. Despite the first part of his title, Frank had very little to do with the newsgathering operations of the paper. He was the face of the *Observer* in the community, making friends and pulling in what few advertising dollars remained for the print media these days. He played a lot of golf, some of which he used to do with SBU's late president, the legendary Father Joe Pirelli.

"Perhaps you can enlighten me as to the identity of that gentleman speaking to Desdemona Bainbridge," Mac said.

Des, wearing a red dress with a plunging neckline that showed off a tattoo of a yellow flower on her chest, stood at the far end of the garden in lively conversation with an aging French gigolo between puffs on her cigarette. At least, he looked like a gigolo to me. I just threw in the French part. He was tall, like Des, with graying fair hair in a ponytail and a three-day growth of beard. His white linen shirt and chinos hung loose on him, as if he'd recently lost weight. I put his age in the mid-sixties.

"That's Gamaliel Taylor, the inaugural artist-in-residence at the Shinkle," Frank said.

Des had a reputation for collecting artists as well as art, but I have to admit I had no real evidence for assuming that Taylor was her latest acquisition. In fact, the difference in their ages was a mark against it. Still . . .

"What kind of art does he do?" I asked Frank.

"Anatomically correct," Mac answered for him. "Kate researched Mr. Taylor's work when his appointment was announced. She is not a devotee of his *oeuvre*."

My sister has opinions about everything, but especially art. Her own specialty is illustrating children's books, and she's quite good at it. Maybe being married to an overgrown child helps.

"Interesting family dynamics with the Bainbridges," Frank mused.

That I knew. Lynda and I had discussed the family trauma drama the evening before during our Friday night cocktail hour. Bartending is one of my jobs as Mrs. Cody's personal assistant.

"As a highly paid PR professional," I'd said then, using one of my standard laugh lines, "I could have told Des that it was a big mistake for her to create what Mac would call a *cause célèbre* out of that chapter about her family in Mitzi Gold's book. She brought more attention to it than it would have had otherwise."

Lynda wrinkled her brows in thought. "I'm not so sure about that. This town runs on gossip the way I run on coffee. Everybody in Erin knew what was in that book before Amazon dropped off the second copy."

"You have me there, especially with the telling details about drugs and father issues and whatnot." Not that I'd read the tome in question, *Family Lies*; I'd learned all this from keeping my ears open during lunches at Daniel's Apothecary and Beans & Books.

"Anyway," Lynda continued, "it was highly unethical for Gold to write about the case, especially without disguising it more. I mean, it's not like the true identity of three adult triplet women and their father designated as 'Family B' in a book written by Erin's only family therapist was a mystery for Sebastian McCabe."

"But at least Gold's therapy seems to have worked. Des should be happy that Bainbridges are all on speaking terms again."

"Maybe not all of them, darling." She sipped her Manhattan, possibly to build the suspense. "I understand that Buckingham Palace isn't big enough to hold Portia and her stepmother at the same time."

"Where did you hear that?"

"Um, I think Polly told me."

"Nuns shouldn't gossip. What else did she say?"

"That Des is the bad girl, Portia is the socialite, and Ophelia is the scholar."

"Everybody in Erin knows that. What's for dinner?"

A sudden halt in the background music at Stratford Court, provided by three talented SBU students and their strings, broke into this reverie of mine and alerted me that something was about to happen. I looked over at the fountain Pan in the center of the garden and saw Ezra Bainbridge being helped to his feet by his wife, Fleur. She was assisted in the task by a thirtyish guy who looked like he just stepped off

a tennis court and a young blonde woman with green eyes
and a face so wholesome she could star in milk commercials,
if there is still such a thing as milk commercials.

"You are looking at Ezra's only grandchild, Goldie,"
Mac informed me in an uncharacteristically low voice,
answering a question I didn't even know I had. "She is
Desdemona's daughter. And, like her, she uses the
Bainbridge surname." Des herself stood more than six feet
away from her father and the others, with the air of a player
on deck and eager to step up to the plate.

"Who's the handsome one?" Lynda asked, curiosity
in her husky voice.

"Who do you mean?" I asked.

She rolled her gold-flecked brown eyes. I couldn't see
that movement behind the sunglasses that hid much of her
lovely oval face, but I've known my Lynda a good chunk of
her soon-to-be-40 years. "The Adonis behind Fleur with the
dark hair, the gorgeous brown eyes, and the trim body," she
specified. "*That* handsome one."

Enough already. I stuck in my stomach. Can I help it if
my wife is an amazing Italian cook, and our gym was closed
for months?

"That's David Gunner of the Bridges Law Firm,"
Frank Woodford said. "He's doing most of the legal work for
the Bainbridge family these days since his father pulled back."

"Must keep him busy," I commented.

At this point I paid attention to the dirty looks around
me and shut up so that we could hear Ezra Bainbridge.
Gripping a portable podium, he spoke feebly, hesitantly, and
none-too-coherently.

"My turn, is it? I want to, uh, welcome you all to
Stratford Court, and, uh . . ." Fleur Bainbridge, a strikingly

pretty woman in her mid-fifties with well-coiffed auburn hair, whispered in his ear. "And thank you for coming. Uh, have a good time. Now Desdemona wants to say something."

She didn't waste any time, moving in before her father had quite moved out. Call me shallow, but I had a hard time ignoring the streak of violet in her long flaxen hair. The rebel in her wasn't dead, though somewhat domesticated.

"Thanks, Dad. I just want to say how thrilled all of our family are to have you here to admire Portia's beautiful flowers, tour our homes, and support the artist-in-residence program at the Shinkle." Somebody started clapping. I'm pretty sure it wasn't me. "Our family put up the seed money for this wonderful program, but we wanted to give all of Erin the opportunity to participate through this fundraiser. Each year from now on a distinguished artist will come to create art *in* Erin, *about* Erin. And I am so pleased to introduce you today to the very first in what we are sure will be a long line of artists-in-residence, Gamaliel Taylor."

This time I did clap, as did we all. Des stepped aside and Taylor took over the podium. Although he was tall, his talk was mercifully short.

"It is good to be back in Erin again. It has been some decades since I was here last, but surprisingly little has changed. I look forward to getting reacquainted. Thank you."

More applause, in inverse proportion to the length of the comments.

"I don't trust him," Lynda whispered.

"I don't trust anybody with that unshaven look." If you're going to have facial hair, you should go all out with a full-face beard like Sebastian McCabe's. And speaking of which, where was Mac? Somehow, he had disappeared during the speechifying. Now that it was over, the student musicians were back on the job with something classical—the Beatles maybe.

"How about another glass of the bubbly?" I asked Lynda.

"Are you trying to get me tipsy, sir?"

"Wouldn't think of it. I'm just trying to justify the ticket cost for this shindig to my inner accountant."

"I should have known."

And so forth.

But before I could find one of the waiters roaming the grounds, Mac returned with Ophelia Bainbridge in tow.

Drink in hand and dressed in a summery green frock, the Bainbridge sister I knew best didn't look particularly like the brainbox that she was. But there wasn't a tattoo in sight and her hair was short, in a no-nonsense look that must have terrified first-year students. She seemed like the sort who was married to her profession, though I heard she had a husband until he drowned in a whitewater rafting accident in Indiana. Apparently, their rows were the stuff of legend.

"I loved your appearance on *Mysteries with McCabe*," Lynda told her.

Launched during the Long Hiatus from physical contact, when people were looking for ways to break up the boredom within four walls, Mac's latest project was a monthly interview conducted over Zoom and broadcast via YouTube. Although Ophelia was not herself a writer of mystery novels, unlike Sebastian McCabe, she reviewed them. She also had a passion for word games, puzzles, anagrams, and the dying message stories of detective-story great Ellery Queen. All of that was grist for Mac's mill. He even quizzed her on *Mysteries with McCabe* about an EQ book that featured a set of triplets in the solution. I'd put out a press release on the episode and touted it on all of SBU's social media accounts just the week before.

Ophelia smiled her thanks to Lynda. "I'm glad that you enjoyed it. So did I. It's always a pleasure to talk about the things that give one pleasure, and your brother-in-law is a skilled interviewer."

"When the subject is interesting," Mac said, "little skill is involved."

I mentally tuned out of this mutual admiration lovefest. But, as communication guru for our little university, I was grateful that our news release had caused *Observer & News-Ledger* education reporter Hadley Reams to write a feature about Ophelia as a mystery maven. And that led, in turn, to a Central News Service story along the same lines, which was great publicity even though CNS isn't exactly the biggest news agency in America.

"Who's your favorite current mystery writer?" Lynda asked.

Was that a twinkle in Ophelia's blue eyes? "You mean other than Sebastian McCabe? This may surprise you, but I confess to a fondness for—"

"What do you mean, not welcome?"

The question was shouted, loud enough to be heard over the music of the violin, viola, and cello. I turned around to see a man I didn't know with a plaid shirt, wire-rim glasses, and unkempt hair standing toe-to-toe with Portia Bainbridge, although she was a little taller.

"Oh, no," Ophelia muttered behind me.

"I'm making a delivery," Plaid Shirt asserted. The words were slightly slurred, which rather undercut the defiant delivery. The man held out a floral bouquet, which struck me as a classic coals-to-Newcastle gesture considering the garden in which he was standing.

I could almost hear Portia counting to 10 inside her head. She removed the chagrin from her face with a visible effort, grabbed the bouquet, and addressed the interloper with a frosty politeness.

"You have completed your task. You may now leave. Officer Lehmann?"

One of Erin's Finest, on private guard duty, stepped from the sidelines. He's a capable officer with little to do on this occasion.

"I'm going, I'm going!" Plaid Shirt assured everybody in the state of Ohio as Lehmann moved in his direction. "You don't have to strongarm me like a freaking fascist."

He departed with an air of injured dignity, walking with exaggerated care.

"It sure is good to be getting together in person again, isn't it?" Lynda said.

Chapter Two
And Thereby Hangs a Tale

That evening, after the kids were down for the night, Lynda looked up and read on the internet the Central News Service story about Ophelia to which she'd originally given scant attention. The CNS headline was "Literature Prof's Pursuits Not Confined to Academia."

By B. U. Melonic

Ophelia Bainbridge is an academic, but not a dry one.

The polymath professor of 20th Century English and American poetry and fiction at St. Benignus University in the small town of Erin, Ohio, is a puzzle fan, a chess player just short of *Queen's Gambit* level, and a reviewer of detective stories for the *Oxford Gazette* under the nom de plume Lia Hope Gabbierdin.

She has also taught a mystery fiction course on "Locked Rooms and Dying Messages" for SBU's popular culture program.

"To the inquiring mind all mysteries are worth exploring," Bainbridge said in an interview, "whether they are to be found in the

works of F. Scott Fitzgerald and William Butler
Yeats or Dorothy L. Sayers and Ellery Queen."

The extensive library at her comfortable
home in Erin, part of a family compound known
as Stratford Court, includes an impressive
collection of Queen's many books. One of the
legendary writers of the so-called Golden Age of
detective fiction, Queen specialized in . . .

"Kind of an odd pen name, isn't it—Lia Hope
Gabbierdin?" Lynda observed.

"It's an anagram for Ophelia Bainbridge."

"How clever of you to figure that out, darling!"

Mac told me.

The rest of the story filled in the details promised by
the first two paragraphs, including Ophelia's membership in
the WASP (Women Armed for Self-Protection, formerly
Women Armed and Set for Peril) gun club, and her lot in life
as a triplet daughter of Ezra Bainbridge.

"She told me the reporter asked enough about her to
write a biography and only used a fraction of it," I reported.
"I think she was half-disappointed he didn't use any of the
info he plied out of her about the family tree and whatnot."

"Well, good on him!" Lynda enthused. "Great
reporters know more than they write and write less than they
know. With Twitter-length attention spans, who reads a 25-
inch story anyway? But do publishers even care today?"

As a self-described recovering journalist, Lynda is
deeply alarmed at what she sees as declining quantity of input
and quality of output in her former profession. Nationally,
newsroom jobs have been shaved by about half over the past
decade as Facebook and Google decimated advertising sales

for newspapers. Many smaller papers have shut down—about a quarter of the U.S. total in the 15 years ended in 2019. I looked that up. On our local scene, the *Observer & News-Ledger's* parent Grier Newspaper Group was struggling under the weight of debt piled up to fend off a corporate raider even before COVID's hit to revenues further reddened its bottom line.

Fortunately for the Cody family finances, the occasional freelance work Lynda still does for the *Observer* and for Grier—a feature article here and a true crime podcast there—takes a back seat to Lynda's budding career as a novelist. Her family saga, *Bluegrass*, was published to good reviews and sufficient sales to stimulate the creative juices for her current project, a generation-spanning newspaper novel called *Ink*. So even in fiction Lynda Teal Cody can't get away from journalism.

"Well, anyway," I said, "this Melonic guy mentioned SBU and spelled our name right. That can't hurt."

I picked up my tablet to resume reading Mac's latest Damon Devlin mystery novel, *Murder With Mirrors*, and didn't give the Bainbridge family another thought until I was forced to later in the week.

"A penny for your thoughts, Boss," said Aneliese Pokorny, handing me my cup of defanged (i.e., sans caffeine) coffee on Thursday morning.

"You'd be overpaying," I quipped.

Now that I was no longer working out of my home office on the screened-in porch of Chez Cody, my indispensable assistant and I were back to the morning banter that helps to fuel our shared day. We needed it as we faced this strange new world. The campus would soon be flooded with students for the first time in more than a year, many of whom had committed to enroll after a virtual visit. Also hitting the campus were fiscal stresses, of which more anon.

Popcorn settled her well-fed, almost 60-year-old body into the chair across my desk—at least six feet across. Her hair was convincingly blond again now that she didn't have to dye it herself. "Do you ever feel like things are normal now, but not really normal?"

I nodded. "I guess this is the new 'new normal.'"

One thing that hadn't changed was the smallness of our operation. Popcorn and I handle all aspects of SBU's marketing, media relations and social media, plus the quarterly alumni magazine, with just the occasional help of an intern and freelancers as needed for special projects. We share an administrative assistant with the alumni office, Popcorn having been promoted out of that role some years earlier. At least government affairs had been taken out of our hands and put into more suitable ones.

"I think I liked the old normal better," Popcorn said. "Heck, in a world where Minnie Cooper is a criminal justice student, anything can happen."

Minnie was a 30-year-old problem child with sticky fingers before being rescued from a life of petty crime by Sister Mary Margaret Malone ("Sister Polly," but Triple M in my mind), Lynda's best gal pal and a member of the campus ministry team at SBU. The delinquent-turned-scholar (?) was top-of-mind that morning because Popcorn and I were working on a media strategy to publicize the criminal justice program's involvement in the Innocence Project. I had shudder-inducing visions of Minnie being interviewed on TV while chain smoking, wearing the SBU-required protective mask as a beard.

My staff (Popcorn) and I had just finished sketching out a plan and timetable for pushing the "students do good" story when Mac called my cell. It was late morning.

"Cody's Circus, clown speaking."

"Good morning, Jefferson. I hope that I am not too late to invite you to lunch. My treat."

"There's no such thing as a free lunch." Mac knows very little about economics. I occasionally try to fill him in, with no discernable success. "What's the catch?"

"Ophelia Bainbridge is seeking our help. How quickly can you get here?"

"Here" was the Beans & Books coffee house and used bookstore on Main Street, which had become a female-oriented art gallery as well after the COVID-induced closing of Looney Ladies. B&B itself had a tough time of it during the worst of the pandemic but was bailed out when a former employee, Beryl Peacock, bought the place with some inherited money and expanded into space next door. At the upper end of the food chain, The Roundhouse fine dinery had closed and rumor said others were holding on by their fingernails. But Paddles & Wheels, the boat and bike rental on Front Street, had to hire more help. It's an ill wind, etc.

I found Mac at a corner table with Ophelia, who was dressed down in shorts and looking stressed.

"It's Portia," the "polymath professor" said by way of explanation as I sat down. "She's accusing Fleur of elder abuse and adultery."

Our approaching server, the always-pleasant Nancy King, must have caught that because she backed off quickly. I mentally backed off myself, stunned by what Ophelia said. On the way there, trying to figure out what was up as I rode my bike the short distance to downtown from the SBU campus, I'd assumed it was some sort of mystery for Mac— not a family drama.

"Elder abuse!" I don't know why that should be any more shocking than the second accusation, but that's what came out of my mouth.

"It does happen, old boy," Mac said. "Remember the sad story of the late Stan Lee."

The legendary Marvel Comics creator, who died at age 95, left behind a legacy of both civil suits and criminal complaints alleging that in his last years he was manipulated and cheated by some of those closest to him. For all I know, that mess may still be winding its way through various courts.

"But it's all bosh!" Ophelia exploded. I don't know whether that's a word Ezra Pound or Robert Frost would have used, but from her it sounded somehow right. "Fleur takes great care of Dad. This is all about Portia never liking her from the day they met. And now Portia's hired an attorney, our WASP friend Phoebe Farleigh, to press this ridiculous claim in court. They're asking for Portia to be made Dad's trustee, with control over all of his medical and financial affairs."

Like David Gunner, Phoebe is the latest generation of an old family firm. Farleigh & Farleigh, founded by her grandfather, handles mostly—but no longer exclusively— civil cases. Presumably, Gunner would be on the other side of any court case, representing Fleur.

"Surely your sister must have something upon which to hang her metaphorical chapeau," Mac said.

"Dad has brain fog, severe fatigue, an erratic heart rate, headaches, and dizziness," Ophelia said. "He has good days and bad days. The fundraiser on Sunday wasn't one of his better days, but I've seen him worse. It's not elder abuse; it's what they're calling 'long COVID,' the aftereffects of the coronavirus. That's happened to probably millions of people, not all of them old, and Dad is eighty-one. We can't blame Fleur for him getting sick."

"Yes, we can," I contradicted. "Or, at least, Portia can. Whether it's true or not."

Before I could elaborate, Nancy King came back to take our orders. "What are we having today?" None of us needed menus. I put in for a tuna salad sandwich on whole wheat, light on the mayo, with Caffeine-Free Diet Coke. Ophelia ordered a salad and Mac reeled off what seemed like about twelve courses.

"Portia could say that your stepmother took Ezra to some super-spreader event without a mask, either out of neglect or deliberately trying to get him sick," I pointed out to Ophelia when we were alone again.

"But she didn't!"

"What about the accusation of adultery?" Mac asked. "That is hardly a legal matter, except as how it might affect the legal affairs of the married couple."

Ophelia looked grim. "It goes to motive, supposedly proving that Fleur isn't a loving wife with her husband's best interests at heart."

"But you don't believe it," I assumed.

"It's absurd. Fleur is with Dad practically every minute. When would she have time for an affair? Portia's so-called evidence is copies of some letters she somehow obtained—letters to Fleur from her first husband, Rory Campbell."

"Written recently?"

"No. They're old letters, but Portia claims the fact that Fleur kept them is proof that she still loves Campbell and is still involved with him."

"Thin gruel indeed," Mac pronounced.

Although I didn't know him, the Campbell name registered in the Cody memory banks.

"Isn't he a doctor?"

Ophelia shook her head. "He hasn't practiced medicine for some years. Now he works for Bruce Gordon's flower shop. He caused quite a disturbance by crashing the party on Sunday, claiming he was making a delivery."

I remembered it well—the shouting, the slurred words. "From doctor to delivery man?"

"I think he does more there than deliver the flowers, Jeff, but your surprise is understandable. He retired early from his medical practice. I believe he has a bit of a drinking problem. The important thing is that the Campbell marriage was over long before Fleur and Dad met at an SBU performance of *Macbeth* about nine years ago" Ophelia smiled at the memory. "After they dated for four months, she handed him an invitation to their wedding and told him he had twenty-four hours to decide. I liked that. Portia didn't."

"So," Mac said, "two sisters with two points of view. That is not unusual."

Ophelia sighed. "It's a little more complicated than that." She paused while our amiable server delivered the goods and quickly vamoosed. Then she went on: "Our sister Des is in Portia's corner." *The boxing image fits!* "I'd like to stub out one of her cigarettes on her chest tattoo." It occurred to me that more family therapy might be appropriate for the Bainbridges, though probably not with Mitzi Gold. This situation had all the makings of a *Midsomer Murders* episode. All it needed was a murder or two.

Mac cleared his throat with all the subtlety of, well, a Mack truck. "And what is it that you wish us to do, Ophelia?"

"I want you to show up at Stratford Court unannounced and observe my father and his interactions with Fleur. Nobody observes more than Sebastian McCabe, except maybe Sherlock Holmes on a good day. And Jeff can be a second witness in case one is needed in court."

My brother-in-law glanced inquiringly at me, but there was no way he was going to say no to that after all the butter she put on it. I gave a slight nod just to feel like my opinion really mattered.

"We would be happy to help," he assured his professorial colleague. Then he turned his attention to the food in front of him. "Shall we say grace?"

Chapter Three
A Serpent's Tooth

Stratford Court lies at the end of a private cul-de-sac in the wealthiest part of Erin. The homes of Ezra Bainbridge and his three daughters, in diverse architectural styles, are arrayed in a circle around a private drive with the family's quarter-acre English garden and its fountain—the scene of Sunday's fundraiser—at the center.

Fleur Bainbridge opened the door of the two-and-a-half-story brick and stucco Tudor mini-mansion, the first house in the circle at Stratford Court. Maybe it was just my imagination that her hazel eyes looked tired before they widened in surprise at the sight of her stepdaughter flanked by Mac and me.

"Sebastian!"

"In the too, too solid flesh, my dear Fleur." *I wish I'd said that.* "You know Jefferson?"

"Only slightly, I'm afraid. What can I do for you?"

"We were talking to Ophelia"—a nod in her direction; let Fleur assume that means we were in the Bainbridge compound during said discussion—"and I had the happy thought of stopping by to say hello to Ezra."

"I'm sure he'll be delighted. Come on in. Fortunately, Ezra is having his best day in weeks. He's in his study, but you can wait in the library."

Of course, Ezra Bainbridge would have both a study *and* a library. He had spent a long lifetime enjoying the fortune compiled by his ancestors over parts of three centuries. He managed his investments (with the help of investment advisor Gulliver Mackie), sat on local non-profit boards (including SBU's), and indulged his passion for the plays of William Shakespeare (or whoever wrote them).

I've been on home tours where "library" meant a room with a few bookcases, some statues swiped from ancient Rome, an antique-looking desk, and chairs more suitable for looking at than sitting in. The library of the Ezra Bainbridge manse, by contrast, had the feel of a scholar's workroom: bookshelves everywhere there wasn't a window, a library table overflowing with opened volumes and notebooks, and the kind of leather wingback chairs that make me want to take up pipe-smoking. The books on the shelves were mostly about Shakespeare and his times, many of them showing signs of use unlike those leather-bound volumes with uncut pages used as decoration.

Mac pointed to a framed photograph on the library table, a lovely brunette who seemed to be making love to the camera with her rich brown eyes. "With all my love, Juliet," was written across the bottom third. Despite the difference in hair color, the woman bore a strong resemblance to the Bainbridge triplets, who favored Ezra not at all. The facial lines and the shape of the nose were similar.

"Your mother?" Mac asked Ophelia. I might almost call his tone of voice tender.

"Yes." She smiled. "My sisters and I never knew her, of course. I wish we had."

There was nothing we could say to that, so Mac just nodded and picked up a hardbacked book called *A Rose by Any Other Name: The Language of Flowers in Shakespeare* by Monica Porlock. The cover had the familiar silhouette of the Bard of Avon superimposed over an image of a single rose.

"I know Monica reasonably well," he said, no surprise, "and I much enjoyed this book some years ago."

"I've heard of the language of flowers, but I don't know much about it," Ophelia said. "I suppose Portia does. She's the flower lover in the family. She and our mother, I guess. Mother painted watercolors of flowers."

"The language of flowers is a rather elaborate system," Mac informed her, "and not as precise as it might be. Many flowers are multivalent. That is, they have different meanings, especially in different cultures." The look on her face said Professor Bainbridge didn't need the definition and was maybe a little insulted by it. "Except for red roses," Mac riffed on. "Roses have been linked to love since Greek mythology. Aphrodite, the goddess of love, emerged from the sea in a shower of foam that transformed into white roses. Later, she became entangled in a rose bush when she went to comfort her dying lover Adonis, and her blood turned the roses red. To this day red roses mean love, although other colored roses can have other meanings. Monica's work, however, is a much broader look at Shakespeare's use of the language of flowers throughout his plays."

Thanks for the book review.

"My knowledge of Shakespeare is no greater than that of an undergraduate English major, unlike my father," Ophelia said for my benefit. "When it comes to poetic dramatists, or dramatic poets, T.S. Eliot is more in my wheelhouse."

Uh-oh. Mac once wrote a journal article—he called it a "monograph"—comparing Don McLean's "American Pie" to the Anglo-American Eliot's "The Wasteland." He could go on forever about Eliot, a fellow Sherlockian.

"Well, that takes us back to roses," Mac said. "Surely you recall the rose imagery that Eliot employed so effectively in 'Ash Wednesday,' part two. How does that go? Ah, yes:

"'Rose of memory
Rose of forgetfulness
Exhausted and life-giving
Worried respectful . . .'"

When he paused for a breath, Ophelia jumped in with:

"'The single Rose
Is now the Garden
Where all loves end
Terminate . . .'"

"Professor McCabe! How good to see you! Just here for a visit, Fleur tells me."

Long COVID hadn't done a thing to mute Ezra Bainbridge's voice. It was strong enough to stop his daughter's poetry recital dead. Somehow her face looked happy without actually smiling when she saw Fleur wheel him in. Despite the heat of an early-August day, Ezra was dressed in a seersucker suit, a pale blue shirt, and a bowtie (also Sebastian McCabe's exclusive neckwear). But then, the house was air-conditioned, and Ezra probably wouldn't be venturing beyond its walls.

"Just a visit," Mac confirmed. "No St. Benignus committee work."

"Good! Then I'll sit in my favorite chair and relax."

Before he could ask, Fleur went to work, lovingly helping him to get out of the wheelchair and into one of the leather wingbacks next to a bust of Master Will. Task accomplished, she hovered beside him, as if poised to take care of any needs. The rest of us settled ourselves into an assortment of comfortable seats.

"I wish I could spend a day prowling your shelves," Mac said.

Ezra seemed to concentrate. "You can, you know. Anytime." He paused, short of breath. "So, why are you really here?"

Mac arched an eyebrow. "Am I that transparent, Ezra?"

The old man's chuckle sounded like a rusty hinge. "Like a window. We've had many a fine discussion over adult beverages, you and I. I've known you for fifteen years, Mac, more or less. And in all that time you've never appealed to me as an SBU board member—and you've never invited yourself to Stratford Court. I can think clearly enough to know I'm not thinking clearly these days, but I'm not completely gaga yet. 'O! Let me not be mad, not mad, sweet heaven! I would not be mad.'[2] So what is it?"

Mac looked at Ophelia, who gave a small nod of approval.

---

[2] Shakespeare's *King Lear*, Act I, Scene 5—*S.McC.*

"Very well, then," he said. "I apologize for the obfuscation. In all candor, I am here at the request of my colleague, Professor Bainbridge, who asked me to come and witness for myself that you are being well treated and not taken advantage of."

Ezra became noticeably agitated, with an expression on his face that was hard to look at—one that said he was trapped in a world not of his making. "I know what this nonsense is about," he said finally. "I'm fine. I have a wonderful wife and everything else I need, except a pair of good legs."

Fleur hugged him and shot Ophelia an unhappy look. "I really wish you'd kept this nasty business in the family," she told her stepdaughter.

"But it's already out of the family," Ophelia reminded her in a tone that was more conciliatory than argumentative. "Since my dear sisters have brought a lawyer into it, there's no way this isn't going to be town gossip. And if it gets to court, I want a respected member of the community well known for his perspicacity to be able to attest that Dad isn't being abused and manipulated by a gold-digger. You know that's what they're saying, Des and Portia."

Fleur sighed. "They never did like me, Ophelia. You know that. I don't know why. You were the only one of the triplets who gave me a chance. I knew I couldn't be your mother at this late date in your lives; I never tried."

Ezra's wide gray eyes wandered, as if he were finding it difficult to focus. They lit on the framed photo. "Juliet," he said. "She's been gone so long, so long. Never knew her girls. I suppose I never knew them, either. I always thought Desdemona was my biggest disappointment, but Portia is the serpent's tooth. 'How sharper than a serpent's tooth it is/To have a thankless child.'[3] Lear was also an old man with three daughters. Nobody knew the human heart like Shakespeare, you know. Across the centuries he still teaches us."

Mac regarded him. "Your hair and fingernails are neatly trimmed, your face shaved. There is nothing slovenly in your dress; in fact, it is impeccable. Your shoes are well shined, for example. I certainly see no indications of mistreatment. There is that troubling matter of lingering COVID symptoms, of course."

"Which my sisters are unfairly blaming on Fleur!" Ophelia exploded.

"He was having telehealth calls regularly with Dr. Abington, and now he's doing it in person," Fleur put in. "The doctor tells me that all of Ezra's symptoms are common in COVID survivors, even relatively young ones."

"Do you have any idea how you contracted the virus?" Mac asked Ezra.

He shrugged his shoulders. "Not specifically. I was a bit more mobile a year ago than I am now. I must have forgotten to wear a mask and keep my distance at some meeting or other."

"I'm still furious with you," Fleur said, looking and sounding like she meant it. "You could have died."

Ezra let loose with another raspy chuckle. "But I didn't, did I? I'm not dead yet and I don't plan to be any time soon."

All of that was shoved to the back of the Cody brain for the next couple of weeks as I went about my professional

---

[3] *Lear* again, Act I, Scene 4—*S.McC.*

business—news releases, arranging interviews, answering media questions, posting on social media, assigning stories for the alumni magazine, and drafting or editing a speech or two. The Bainbridge clan was off my radar for the most part, except for catching the occasional whisper here and there that the family's lawyers were earning their pay. I only found out later that Mac called Dr. Thomas Abington the day of our visit to Stratford Court but the medico refused on ethical grounds to even confirm that Ezra was under his care.

Late on the evening of Tuesday, August 17, the day after SBU's fall term began with the first in-person classes in more than a year and a COVID-delayed memorial Mass for our late president Father Pirelli, my energies turned happily to activities that are none of your business. And that's when my cell rang. It's never off and I always answer it because a communications director is always on the clock. Lynda peered over my shoulder and saw who was calling.

"Aurelia Banfield," she read. "That can't be good."

"Tell me something I don't know, my sweet."

Not that I don't like the assistant chief of the St. Benignus University Police (SBUP, aka campus security). *Au contraire*, as Mac would say. I think Banfield's the bee's knees—smart, grounded, and so brave she calls Sebastian McCabe "Seb." But I knew this wasn't a social call; she would have texted me if she just wanted to know if I'd bought my SBU Lady Dragons season tickets yet.

I answered the phone with a jovial, "Who died?" instead of my name.

After a pause that I later realized was that "stunned silence" you've read about in books, she finally said, "Ophelia Bainbridge. How did you know somebody died?"

"I was just being a smartass."

"Oh."

"And now I feel like an asshole." That was no overstatement. I had a sudden vision of Ophelia as I last saw her, trying to fight what she regarded as an unjust accusation against her stepmother. "This is awful. What happened?"

"She was murdered—blunt force trauma to her head. Jack just told me. I thought you'd want to know because Dr. Bainbridge was a faculty member."

The imperturbable Lt. Col. L. Jack Gibbons, right-hand man to Erin Police Chief Oscar Hummel, is smitten with Banfield. In fact, I once saw him almost smile in her direction when he thought no one was looking.

"I appreciate the call," I said. "What else can you tell me?"

"The victim's niece, Goldie Bainbridge, found the body when she stopped for a visit. Apparently, the younger Ms. Bainbridge lives nearby and does that a lot. *Did* that a lot. Jack says the Chief thinks it's a simple case of burglary gone wrong and not, quote, 'Mac's kind of case.' Well, that's all I know. I'll let you get back to whatever you were doing."

You've kind of spoiled the mood for that, Banfield.

I thanked her, wished her a pleasant evening, and disconnected.

"Do you think Oscar's right about it being a burglary?" Lynda asked, having overheard.

"I don't know, but it would make a nice change of pace. And yet, I wonder if her sisters have alibis. Their case against Fleur just got a little easier with Ophelia out of the way."

"That's an awful thing to say!"

"You're right. Forget I said it."

Chapter Four
Murder Most Foul

The body was discovered too late in the day to make the Wednesday morning print edition of the *Observer & News Ledger*, but Tall Rawls had a brief story in the *Online Observer* under the headline "Professor Found Dead in Home." It began:

> The body of Ophelia Bainbridge, a St. Benignus University professor and scion of one Erin's wealthiest families, was found yesterday at her home by a niece. Police say she was struck in the head by an expensive bookend made of alabaster marble.
>
> "We're treating this as homicide, not an accident," said Oscar Hummel, Erin chief of police. "Most likely she interrupted a burglary in progress." He declined to give details to support that theory, noting that the investigation is in its earliest stages.
>
> Bainbridge, 42, one of three triplet daughters of philanthropist Ezra Bainbridge, was a respected academic who also reviewed mystery fiction under the pseudonym . . .

"You would think that a place like Stratford Court would have hot and cold running security alarms all over the place, if not their own full-time security patrol to keep the bad guys out," I mused to Popcorn.

"Oscar said you'd be surprised how many people, even rich ones, buy security systems but don't bother to turn them on," she informed me.

"Is that the kind of thing you and the Chief talk about on dates?"

"What makes you think we talk?"

Knowing a good exit line when she uttered one, she exited. I resumed my interrupted work on a press release about the tragic death of our faculty member. Lesley Saylor-Mackie, SBU's executive vice president and provost who had once been the deceased's dean, provided this gem of a quote: "Dr. Bainbridge was that rare combination of distinguished scholar, popular teacher, and accessible writer. Our faculty is much diminished by her loss." The best part was that Saylor-Mackie didn't say "She will be missed," which is one of my least favorite pointless clichés.

I was down to the final paragraph of the story, listing the titles of Ophelia's books (*The Love Song of T.S. Eliot* being the most memorable, in my opinion), when Grant Kingsley popped into my office. Since he descended to my turf, not summoning me upstairs to his, I knew this was to be an informal conversation. But that didn't stop me from wanting to salute when he came through the door. Despite more than two years of service as interim president and now president of SBU, and a turn as senior vice president of the Altiora Corp. before that, GK still exhibits the military bearing of his 27 years in the U.S. Air Force. His steel gray hair remains military-short. He was just past his 61st birthday that summer, but I figured he still had a long run ahead in the president's office.

"I just talked to Ezra Bainbridge," he informed me as he sat down. I didn't tell him he was in Popcorn's chair. "That was a tough call."

"How is he holding up?"

"He isn't. The conversation only lasted a few minutes before his wife had to take over." He held up a hand, as if to ward off an objection I hadn't made. "I don't mean 'took over' in a bad way. I know there's been some gossip around her care of Ezra, or lack thereof, but she seemed okay to me. He hasn't been the same since he contracted COVID, but I don't buy the idea that's her fault. Fortunately, to be frank, his main service to the board has always been his family name and his genuine devotion to the institution." GK allowed himself a smile as he added: "And his generosity. Anyway, Jeff, I read what the *Online Observer* reported about the murder. What didn't they report? What's the inside story?"

"There isn't one, so far as I know. Since Oscar thinks Ophelia's murder was a bungled burglary, Mac isn't involved and probably won't be."

He frowned, telegraphing his disappointment. GK has a childish interest in both the mystery novels and the real-life cases of Sebastian McCabe. You would think our president had enough to worry about in this post-pandemic world, what with 2021 enrollment still lagging after a 4 percent slide last year (16.1 percent for freshmen), global students falling off the charts, and talk of doctoral programs having to be cut. About the only good news is that we weren't big enough or select enough to have an admissions scandal like the one that roped in all those Hollywood types in 2019.

"Well," GK said, standing up, "Dr. Bainbridge and her father are both valued members of the SBU family, so I'm interested. Let me know if Mac does get mixed up in it."

"I am afraid, old boy, that I have been asked to look into Ophelia's murder," Mac told me on the phone a few hours later.

Since when does "afraid" mean "deliriously happy"?

"Asked by whom?"

"Ezra Bainbridge. According to Fleur, who just called me, he refuses to believe that Ophelia's murder was the result of a burglary."

"Isn't that just the babbling of a confused old man in denial?"

"Possibly. Nevertheless, I am going to Stratford Court right now. Care to join me?"

I told Popcorn where I was going on my way out.

"Oscar won't like that," she said.

"I'm not sure I like it myself. But GK will. That reminds me." I sent our president a quick text: *Ezra Bainbridge asked Mac to investigate.* He sent back a thumbs up sign.

Ezra and Fleur Bainbridge weren't alone in their home. Ezra's blonde granddaughter, Goldie, and the young lawyer David Gunner were there as well. Goldie hovered over the old man while Fleur and Gunner stood to one side.

"Thank you for coming," Fleur told Mac. "Ezra was very insistent."

"Words are inadequate to express all of one's emotions at a time like this," Mac said. "I can only assure you of my sorrow, my sympathy, and my willingness to help the Bainbridge family in any way that I can."

Goldie, in her mid-twenties, looked like she hadn't slept since she found the body the night before. "This is a nightmare," she said. "I just want to wake up."

Her grandfather looked up at her with untold sorrow in his aged eyes, and I wasn't sure who was comforting whom, or if any comfort was possible.

"The police—" Gunner began, reminding me that he was there. But Ezra interrupted.

"You know what I want, Sebastian," he said in a firm voice. "Find the man—or woman—who killed my Ophelia."

"Surely Chief Hummel and his officers are competent to do that," Mac demurred. Gunner mentally nodded; I could feel it. "Their resources are greater than mine."

"Not their mental resources if they think some common burglar did this. Tell him, Goldie."

"I know Aunt Ophelia's house like I know my own, Professor McCabe. I drop by a lot just to hang out. When COVID got hot last year, we formed a bubble. Anyway, the place is full of valuable artworks. But the only thing the killer took was some jewelry from her bedroom. And more drawers were pulled out than necessary, as if to make damned sure it looked like the work of a thief who was searching for something saleable."

Mac raised an eyebrow. "That is highly perceptive of you, Miss Bainbridge."

Goldie gave a weak smile. "I read your Damon Devlin mysteries. Anyway, there's something more." She closed her eyes, took a breath, and soldiered on. "Aunt Ophelia was hit in the head with a marble bookend in an art deco design that was worth more than all but a few pieces of her jewelry. Why didn't the burglar take that instead of leaving it behind?"

"It would have been hard to fence," Gunner said, beating me to it.

The look Goldie gave him was hard to read, but it might have been exasperation.

"You could sell it on eBay right now—or a few months from now when the heat is off—for fifteen hundred dollars," she countered. "That's not a fortune to this family, but it would buy a lot of drugs. A professional burglar would have known that, and an amateur would have taken more."

Somebody had to play devil's advocate here, and Mac decided that it would be him:

"Most likely Oscar will posit that Ophelia interrupted the burglar, causing him to strike her and then flee in a panic."

"Then why wipe his fingerprints off the bookend and leave it behind instead of taking it with him and tossing it in the Ohio River?" Goldie said. "Colonel Gibbons, who was my volleyball coach in junior high, told me on the phone this morning that there were no prints on the murder weapon. And we haven't even talked about how the killer got in. You know there was no forced entry, right?"

The look on Ezra's face told me that he was struggling without success to follow all this, but he had a firm grasp on his bottom line:

"You have to investigate this, Sebastian."

"Very well, then." *Throw me into that briar patch.* "I am compelled to ask the obvious questions first. Did Ophelia have an amorous attachment?"

"He means, a lover," I translated.

They all shook their heads, but I knew that wasn't a question he would let loose of; he'd ask others as well, because Ophelia's relatives might be in the dark about her love life, if any.

"And who inherits her estate?" Mac directed that one to Gunner.

"I can't answer that question. It would be unethical."

"I inherit almost everything," Goldie supplied without so much as a glance at Gunner. "The exception is the specified amounts bequeathed to the university, Serenity House, and a few other charities. Aunt Ophelia told me. I never thought . . ." She stopped.

Mac sighed. "Very well. Love and money are ruled out, at least for now. I would like to visit the scene of the murder."

But that didn't happen. Ophelia's domicile, a single-story, mid-century modern home in sharp contrast to Ezra's Tudor manse across the circle on the other side of the English garden, was surrounded by crime scene tape. That was no bar to Sebastian McCabe when Oscar invited him into a case, but this was different.

"Sorry, Professor, no can do," said Officer Mentzel, declining to let us in. "Orders from headquarters." If there's one thing Mentzel is good at, it's taking orders.

An orange tabby cat curled about his feet.

"Is that the victim's cat?" I asked him.

"Yup!"

"Doubtless the cat who did nothing in the night-time," Mac said. "Given the hypothesis that Ophelia did not interrupt a burglary in process, then there was no screeching of a discommoded feline to alert her to such."

"That reminds me," I said, "if that killer wasn't a burglar but wanted to look like one, why didn't he fake a break-in?"

"A very astute question, Jefferson! However, do not discount the most obvious and likely explanation."

"That being?"

"Incompetence, aggravated by lack of experience at homicide."

"You guys are overcomplicating this," Oscar said. "Java?"

The question was highly rhetorical, seeing as how Mac was already pouring himself a cup of caffeinated pleasure from the Keurig machine into the ceramic **I SEE NO REASON TO ACT MY AGE** mug the Chief keeps on hand for Mac's not-infrequent visits.

Oscar sat back with a satisfied smile on his broad face, looking Buddha-like. "I don't think my crack team needs your help on this one, Mac, thank you very much."

"And, therefore, we were denied access to the crime scene. That chaffed, Oscar; after all these years, I must say that chaffed."

"You mean my officers followed the law?" Perhaps in response to the hurt look on Mac's face—an excellent piece of acting, if I'm any judge—Oscar changed his tone, but not his tune. "Look, I've bent the law plenty of times to let you guys go under crime scene tape—"

"When you needed us to solve the case for you," I put in.

"When I was on the scene myself," Oscar corrected, not very convincingly. "But I'm not comfortable letting you run wild when I'm not there." *Yeah, that's us: wild.* "This has nothing to do with the fact that you are—let me repeat—overcomplicating this with your not-burglary theory."

"Nevertheless, may I presume you have no objection to Jefferson and I making a few inquiries in our usual fashion?" Mac said.

"Inquire away."

"Very well, then. I will begin with you. Under your theory, how did the burglar get in the house?"

"The victim kept a key under the flowerpot on her front porch."

"How do you know that?"

"It's still there."

Even Mac's substantial beard couldn't conceal his skepticism. "Do you suppose the burglar returned it? After wiping his fingerprints off the fatal bookend?"

"How the hell do you know there were no prints?"

"We have our sources," I tossed off. "Answer the question."

"I don't pretend to have all the answers yet." Who could blame him for sounding a bit sullen? He had a bad hand to play, and he was trying not to know it. "Our investigation is less than fifteen hours old. The victim's niece called it in at seven forty-three last night. She stopped by after dinner, which apparently wasn't unusual."

"I presume it is too soon to estimate the time of death?" Mac asked.

"A trained investigator never presumes," Oscar said. He must have enjoyed delivering that line. "Eppensteiner"—that's Dr. Arlene "Arly" Eppensteiner, Sussex County Coroner—"put a rush on the autopsy. Probably because of the victim's last name, but you didn't hear me say that.

Anyway, she said from the state of rigor it was pretty clear the victim died just two or three hours before the body was found."

"In the afternoon, then—an odd time indeed for a burglary!" Having made that point and gotten no rise out of Oscar, Mac changed the subject. "I gather the burglar alarm did not go off when the miscreant entered."

"Miss Bainbridge was at home. Who turns on the burglar alarm when they're at home and they haven't gone to bed yet?"

I do. Then Lynda sets it off when she remembers to put something in the recycling bin after dinner.

Instead of answering, Mac grabbed that petard and tried to hoist Oscar on it. "Not only was Ophelia in residence, Oscar, but that fact would have been obvious to any thief in search of easy plunder. Her automobile, a late-model red Honda Acura, was in the driveway rather than in the garage. I observed that this morning. Ohio license plate number AGD 3678." *Show off.* "What burglar would enter a home when the owner was there?"

Oscar squirmed in his chair. "I never said we're dealing with Raffles here. People do crazy things when they're desperate for drugs, and COVID made the opioid crisis worse."

"What about Ophelia's gun?" I asked.

"How do you know she had a gun?"

"She was a member of WASP—that was in the wire service story about her. Most of those gals are carrying when they go to the dentist. So why didn't she grab her gun when she went to confront the burglar?"

"He wasn't a dentist."

"Well done, Oscar!" said Mac. "You are developing a certain vein of pawky humor."

"Eh?"

"Don't encourage him," I advised.

"Look," Oscar said, "let's get real-world here. Ms. Bainbridge probably had her gun stored in some safe place where she couldn't reach it in time. Or she thought the noise she heard was the cat knocking over something."

"Not implausible," Mac admitted. "May we see the crime scene photos?"

With a grunt, Oscar pulled up a whole series of them on his computer, showing Ophelia stretched out on her living room floor from various angles.

"As you can see, she was hit from behind," Oscar said.

"That flower by her hand!" Mac exclaimed, pointing. It was a pretty thing, bell-shaped and bright yellow like Lynda's old Mustang.

"What about it?" Oscar said.

"It looks as though Ophelia might have been grasping it before it fell out of her hand in her death throes. If so, that must mean something. The flower is a columbine, undoubtedly from the garden at Stratford Court."

"Yeah, undoubtedly. But you're making something out of nothing. She was probably just sticking it in the vase when she was hit. There's a crystal vase on the table near here; you can see it in that picture."

"Come, come, Oscar, that hardly fits with your surprised burglar scenario!" He rubbed his facial forest, a sure sign that the McCabe mind was at work. "Far more likely, in the last few moments of her life Ophelia Bainbridge took the columbine *out* of that vase after the killer left as she sought to tell us who killed her."

"That only happens in books," Oscar protested.

"To be precise, it happens in books of exactly the kind that Ophelia loved—those from the aptly named Golden Age of the detective story. She collected the works of Ellery Queen, who excelled in the conceit of the 'dying message' left by the victim to point to the murderer in such works as Queen's *The Siamese Twin Mystery*. It is not only plausible but likely that she would attempt to emulate that stratagem if at all possible."

"But that's—"

"Confirmation bias," stuck in Holly Burdette, Oscar's executive assistant, on her way to a filing cabinet. About Goldie Bainbridge's age, with copper-colored hair in a pixie cut and pearl earrings, she is working on a master's degree in criminal justice in her spare time.

Mac arched an eyebrow at her. "Would you care to elaborate on that observation?"

"I think you've subconsciously decided that there ought to be a dying message, so that's why you see one there," Holly said. "Like in your Damon books *Hocus-Pocus* and *Nothing Up My Sleeve*."

In response, Mac buried his face in his mug. I can't be sure, but I think he was smiling.

"You checked Ophelia's cell phone, didn't you, to see if there was anything interesting like a threat?" I said.

Oscar frowned. "We haven't been able to get into it yet."

"Try applying Ophelia's thumb print," Mac suggested. "Sometimes biometrics works even when the thumb is part of a dead body."

Really? I can hardly ever get my thumbprint to open my phone, and I'm alive.

"I'm sure Gibbons is on it," Oscar said. He chugged coffee. "But if the killer wasn't an inept burglar, what's the motive?"

"The usual reasons are money or sex or both," Holly told him, stating the obvious. Or maybe she learned that in one of her classes.

The Chief gave that a self-satisfied smile. "From what I can tell, Ms. Bainbridge had been living a nun-like existence since the death of her husband some years back. And money takes us right back to a burglar, which is right where we should be, dying message be damned."

"For whatever it may be worth," Mac said, "I call your attention to tensions within the Bainbridge family. You may recall that their contentious interactions became local gossip fodder because of an unfortunate book by their family therapist. And now they are in the midst of a new fracas that has pitted Ophelia and her stepmother against the other two Bainbridge triplets."

Oscar got up and put a new cartridge in the coffee maker. "Rich people like the Bainbridges don't kill each other; they sue each other. Trust me, Mac, you're barking up the wrong tree without a paddle on this one."

Chapter Five
Much Ado

"I love my Oscar," Popcorn said, back at the office, "but I'd never, ever bet against Sebastian McCabe."

"I wouldn't either," I said, "but even the pope isn't infallible."

"Actually, Jeff, he is."

"Only in matters of doctrine. He can be wrong about who's going to win the Kentucky Derby. But never mind that. Getting back to Oscar, I imagine he's a little skittish dealing with the likes of the Bainbridges. Between them, they sit on every important board in town and donate a lot of money to the prosecutor's campaigns. That means that Slade is going to be pushing Oscar especially hard on this one."

"I'm sure that has nothing to do with Oscar's theories about the murder."

Time to change the subject!

"Didn't you say our new intern is here?"

"Yep. Caffeinated and ready to go."

A senior drama major named Riley St. Simon, the energetic intern had magenta hair in pigtails, denim overalls, and lots of ideas about promoting the upcoming production of *The Music Man* at SBU's Davenport-Lattimer Bijou Theatre—the first in-person performance after a year of livestreaming. I set her loose on that, under Popcorn's tutelage, along with a number of less glamorous but equally necessary office chores during that first week of the semester.

After an hour or so of tending to my own knitting, an idea about that columbine flower at the murder scene grabbed hold of me and wouldn't let go. I found myself wandering over to Mac's fire trap of an office in Herbert Hall. I found him juggling three eggs.

"Juggling?" I uttered.

Mac kept his eyes on the task at hand, not looking at me. "It is always good to learn new skills, old boy, and I understand that learning to juggle accelerates the growth of neural connections related to focus, memory, and vision, plus builds eye-hand coordination in a way that not only improves reaction time, but also reflexes, spatial awareness, concentration, and strategic thinking."

Say that again real fast.

"Well, I'm sure you could use all of that, but you're juggling eggs!"

"Worry not, old boy! These are magic eggs." With that, he caught two eggs in one hand and one in the other, clapped the hands together, and produced instead of a yolky mess a stream of silk handkerchiefs of various hues. Disappointed and therefore cranky—because I expected doves—I said:

"So, I came over to talk to you about that columbine at Ophelia's place."

Mac sat behind the mountain of papers and books that hid his desk, clearly longing to light a forbidden cigar. "I have learned a lot about that species of flora since I saw you last, Jefferson. In Italian *commedia dell'arte*, Columbine is the love interest of Harlequin. However, the flower apparently takes its English name from the Latin *columbinus,* meaning "dove-like," from *columba* for dove, upon the theory that the inverted flower resembles a cluster of five doves."

"I would say it's bell-shaped."

"What the plant looks like is clearly in the eye of the beholder. For example, the Latin name for the plant is *Aquilegia,* derived from the Latin word for eagle, *aquila,* on the premise that the spurs extending behind the flower petals resemble the claws of an eagle."

"Fascinating, I'm sure, but unless Ophelia was killed by a dove or an eagle—"

"I have also learned that one must not overwater the columbine plant, and that one can extend the blooming season as much as six weeks into mid-summer by deadheading the fading plant, which the Stratford Court gardener apparently did. It may interest you, as it did me, that seeds and roots of the plant historically have been used to treat a range of ailments including heart problems, sore throats, and headaches. Native Americans used the crushed seeds as a love charm as well as for medicinal purposes."

"What does all that have to do with Ophelia Bainbridge?"

"Almost certainly nothing."

"Well, I have an idea that might: The language of flowers."

Mac arched an eyebrow. "Indeed?"

"Ophelia was naming her killer using the language of flowers!"

He curbed his enthusiasm.

"Do you recall her words to us on that subject, Jefferson? 'I've heard of the language of flowers, but I don't know much about it.'"

"That was two weeks ago, plenty of time for her to have read that book in her father's library and learned *all* about it."

"Indeed she could have, I must concede. And if she did, what meaning did she find ascribed to columbine that she wished to leave as a clue to her killer?"

"I didn't get that far," I admitted. "I just thought of this about ten minutes ago."

"As it happens, Jefferson, I did get that far." His flipper of a right hand fished around the chaos of his desk and pulled up the familiar volume: *A Rose by Any Other Name: The Language of Flowers in Shakespeare* by Monica Porlock.

I felt myself get hot under the collar, and not just figuratively. My neck must have been red with anger.

"If you had all this doped out already, why didn't you say so to begin with instead of letting me make a fool out of myself?"

"A fool? Hardly, old boy! You reasoned exactly as I did. Bravo! That path was a dead end, however, which is why I saw no need to start there in relating to you my morning's mental work. Here is Monica on the meaning of columbine. I looked it up in the index: 'This beautiful plant has almost as many meanings as it has petals on its flower. It can, for example, mean folly or foolishness, drawn from the resemblance of the flower to the hat of a court jester.'"

"At least that's not another comparison to a bird," I interjected.

Mac nodded and continued quoting from his friend Porlock: "'That may be Ophelia's meaning when she says, "There's fennel for you and columbines." Or she may mean to indicate flattery or insincerity. On the other hand, columbine has also been seen as a symbol of fortitude.'"

He looked up. "Monica refers here to the character Ophelia in Shakespeare's *Hamlet*. She quotes from the famous 'madness scene' in that play:

> "'There's rosemary, that's for remembrance:
> pray you, love, remember: and there is pansies,
> that's for thoughts.
> There's fennel for you, and columbines:
> there's rue for you; and here's some for me:
> we may call it herb of grace o' Sundays: O
> you must wear your rue with a difference.
> There's a daisy: I would give you some violets,
> but they withered when my father died:'"

All Greek to me!

"What the hell!" I exploded. "If the flower Ophelia Bainbridge grabbed when she died is a call back to Will Shakespeare's Ophelia, then it seems even more like a clue. But something that can mean so many different things in effect means nothing at all. Columbine leaves us clueless!"

"You have seized the point exactly, Jefferson! It is hard to believe that Ophelia would leave such a multivalent message." He didn't stop to explain multivalent again. "The flower must mean something else, something more general."

"Such as?"

"Is there someone associated with Ophelia whose name is a flower?"

"You're asking me? You would know better than I whether there's a Lily or an Iris or a Jasmine in her life," I pointed out. "You were her friend and colleague."

"I know of none. Of course, Fleur is French for 'flower.' Ophelia's French was excellent."

Sex or money, I thought, uninterested in the late professor's linguistic skills.

"Fleur is quite a bit younger than her husband and has been accused of cheating on him as well as neglecting him," I pointed out. "Sounds like a Class A suspect to me."

"Why would she kill the only one of her three stepdaughters who was in her corner?"

Oh. "What a minute! That's right! I thought of it earlier: Ophelia's death removes an obstacle to Portia and Des. And Des has a yellow flower tattooed on her chest!" *I gave it a good look.*

"Excellent thought, old boy! That is certainly worth pursuing. As is Lucius Snedeker."

"Snedeker?"

"The Stratford Court gardener. Given that the columbine—"

My phone rang.

"Hi, Jeff, this is Cindy Weller, from the *Spectator.*"

I try to treat student reporters from the campus paper with the same respect I give the *Observer* and Morrie Kindle of the AP, so I turned my back on Mac and focused. After several seconds of reporter-to-source chatter, she asked me if it was true that several departments—music, philosophy, and comparative literature, to name names—would be pausing admissions after the current academic year.

"It would be premature to say so definitively, Cindy," I advised her. "But that step is under consideration at the department level. SBU, like many universities around the country, is prioritizing those students who have already matriculated in order to give them . . ."

And so forth. I gave it to her reasonably straight, skipping only GK's rather colorful language about the plethora of Ph.D's on the unemployment lines.

"Thanks, Jeff," she said at the end. "Hey, I was really sorry to hear about the murder of Professor Bainbridge. She was one of my favorite profs last year."

"You have a lot of company on that."

"So, is this going to be one of those deals where Professor McCabe solves the murder and you're like his Watson?"

"I'm not his Watson!"

"Oh, I'm sorry." She actually sounded like it. "What are you, then?"

Whoever said there's no such thing as a stupid question was stupid. "I'm his Jeff Cody. And I'm good at it."

Chapter Six
No More Cakes and Ale

"I'd better get back to work," I huffed at Mac after disconnecting from the still-apologetic Cindy Weller. "I can't hang around here spit-balling ideas with you all day."

Even though I often do.

"Have you had lunch?" Mac asked.

"Not yet."

He stood up. "Then you had best do so. It is almost one-thirty. Shall we go to Daniel's?"

"Maybe not. I'm still trying to lose the fifteen pounds I picked up during lockdown."

"Depriving your brain of the nourishment it needs does not strike me as a good tactic. You have redoubled your efforts to visit the gymnasium several days a week, have you not? I thought so. You will be back in shape in no time, old boy. No need to starve yourself!"

Sebastian McCabe, who is approximately a hundred pounds overweight and broke his leg the one time he tried to work out,[4] was giving me weight loss advice. I resisted his siren song to lunch until he once again uttered those two magic words: "My treat."

---

[4] See *Too Many Clues*, MX Publishing, 2019.

Pandemics may come and go, but Daniel's Apothecary stays firmly rooted in approximately 1959, although the various generations of the Daniel family have been serving up prescriptions on one side of the building and food on the other since 1904. The menu, the décor, and the jukebox emphasize the icons of my father's youth. On this particular day, as on so many others, I ordered an "Elvis" sandwich—peanut butter and banana—while sitting under a poster of Marilyn Monroe and looking at a Route 66 clock. With some wistfulness, I recalled all the times I had met Lynda here for lunch when she worked next door at the *Observer*. And in my imagination, I could see the faces of several elderly lunch-counter habitués of my acquaintance who had been carried off by COVID. No more cakes and ale for them. (I speak symbolically, "cakes and ale" meaning the good things of life; Daniel's is more of an apple pie and milkshake kind of place.)

"As I was saying before we were so rudely interrupted by that phone call," Mac told me, "the flower as a clue could have been referring to the Bainbridge gardener, Lucius Snedeker. He must have given the columbine some special attention to keep it blooming this late in the year."

"What motive would Snedeker have?"

"Perhaps Ophelia caught him doing something nefarious."

"Like stealing fertilizer for his own use?" I shook my head. "I still prefer Des with her tattoo."

"It is the wrong flower, old boy, a marigold."

"But the right color!" Behind all that beard, Mac's face looked pained at this observation. "All right, then," I persisted, "what about Portia? The flower could point to her.

She likes flowers. Fred Gaffe once told me that she spends a lot of time with the gardener."

Mac raised an eyebrow. "Perhaps it is not only the flowers that she likes."

"Well, whatever gets her to the garden, a flower clue might point to Portia."

"The notion is not to be dismissed out-of-hand, I concede. It seems to me that you have focused on a likely suspect and found a way to make the clue match. Perhaps that is not a bad idea. Who else would make a good suspect?"

"Ophelia's husband would," I said, "except for the inconvenient fact that he's dead. What was his name?"

"Devan O'Rourke, a poet and novelist—albeit one of very minor talent."

"I remember him, hon," said our server, Vern, setting down Mac's "Fats Domino Burger" and my "Elvis." Shaped like the Pillsbury doughboy and just as cheerful, she calls everybody "hon" even though she knows our names. "He used to come here for breakfast sometimes, usually hung over. He must have thought poets with Irish names were supposed to drink a lot. Didn't he drown about five years ago while he was having an argument with his wife?"

"That is reasonably accurate, I believe," Mac said. "Ophelia was devastated."

This marital style sounded uncomfortably like Lynda's parents, who divorced years ago but remain friends with benefits when they aren't yelling at each other.

Vern moved on.

"Ruling out the husband due to death," I resumed, "the Bainbridges said Ophelia didn't have a romantic attachment. But they might not know, given all the drama there." I brooded. "And even if they did, what if there was something scandalous about this theoretical love interest? They wouldn't talk about it. Old money likes to pretend that any family dirt is just fertilizer for orchids." I was getting carried away by all the flower talk. "I miss the Old Gaffer. He knew things about people they didn't know about themselves."

"May he rest in peace! In his absence, perhaps Frank Woodford can fill a similar role."

Chapter Seven
At One Fell Swoop

We got more out of our visit next door at the *Observer* than we expected.

Serena Mason, who has a heart of gold and pockets lined with the same material, was just leaving the offices as we approached. She's medium height, in her seventies, with very short hair more salt than pepper. Philanthropy is her day job as she distributes her late husband's family fortune to numerous good causes, but she also has been known to putter in business with more than mediocre success.

"Oh, hello there," she said as she caught sight of us.

"Good afternoon, Serena," Mac said. Everybody calls her Serena. "What brings you calling on the Fourth Estate today?"

"Oh, you know, just dropping by. How about you? What's on your agenda today?"

"We're poking into the death of Ophelia Bainbridge," I said, cutting to the chase.

I was glad she wasn't wearing a protective mask so that I could enjoy the expression of surprise on her face. "Whatever for? That was a common burglary gone wrong, wasn't it? Hardly your kind of thing."

"That is certainly Oscar's rather stubbornly held point of view," Mac conceded. "Whether he is correct remains to be seen. Quite possibly there was a more personal motive for the murder."

Serena quickly added two and two, and there was nothing wrong with her math. "So, you're here to see what the local press can tell you, any personal or family secrets. And you'll be talking to Frank Woodford because he's been around forever, as well as being managing director of the paper with his ear to the ground."

"Mostly on the golf course," I said. "That's the ground his ear is usually on when the weather is nice."

"And he's no duffer," she said dryly. "I know. Anyway, you're going to ply Frank for unpublished intel about the Bainbridge family."

Mac tacitly admitted as much by not denying it. On the other hand, he didn't volunteer the information that Ezra Bainbridge invited us into the investigation. "Do you know the family well yourself?" he asked. "We saw you at the Stratford Court fundraiser for the Shinkle Museum of Art."

"I think I know them about as well as I'd want to, even though Ezra is a fine man and my late husband's sixth cousin or something of the sort. But I was at that garden party because I've always supported the Shinkle. So have the Bainbridge sisters, of course, each for different reasons. Desdemona has always lived as much like a bohemian artist as one can with family money and a house at Stratford Court, while Portia likes being seen with people who like to be seen. I knew Ophelia least of all, and certainly not well enough to shed any light on a possible murder motive, although she did contribute to Serenity House."

The Mason Foundation is one of the major funders of Serenity House, which supports homeless women and children with a range of services. Serena is board chair, and there are those who think the organization was named for her. Lynda and Kate both volunteer there.

"I certainly hope her murderer is caught and justice is done," Serena added.

"We can but try," Mac told her.

The conversation petered out quickly after that. My favorite philanthropist wished us a good day, told us to give her love to our spouses, and went on her way. Mac followed her with his eyes.

"Evasive, was she not, Jefferson?"

"I wouldn't say that. I think she made her feelings about each of the sisters quite clear."

"I was referring to her visit to the *Observer*. When I inquired the nature of her call, she answered in the vaguest possible terms and then turned the question back on us. I wonder what she was trying to hide?"

"That's just confirmation bias," I advised him. "You're so used to people evading and lying that you find it when it's not even there. I hope that doesn't extend to pillow talk at your house."

Mac started to say something, thought better of it, and instead silently led the way into the familiar territory of the *Observer* offices.

We found Frank Woodford with his feet on his desk in a none-too-happy mood. He'd moved back into his old office, the one from which he'd been evicted to make room for Lynda when she was editorial director for Grier Ohio NewsGroup—a position that no longer exists.

"Corporate keeps cutting costs, mainly employees, because revenues are tanking," he complained after the usual round of social greetings. "Have been for about twenty years.

Social media advertising is eating our lunch. That's not likely to change unless those anti-trust suits filed by newspapers against Google and Facebook succeed."

I sensed that Frank wouldn't want to be reminded that his little paper was just a cog in a much bigger wheel and a more complicated story, which involved the old Grier Media Corp. spinning off the newspaper operations into a separate (and perennially unprofitable) company as part of a defense against an Austrian takeover tycoon known as the Tin Man. Recalling that fiasco, and what happened to the price of Grier stock, I zoned out a little on Frank's jeremiad. When I tuned back in, he was saying:

". . . digital. Except for Megan Whitlock, most of the higher-ups don't have newspaper ink in their veins like I do. They really only care about the digital product because it generates more profit—no cost of ink, paper, and delivery to cover. It means nothing to them that the *Observer* was started by a printer in 1836 and only became part of Grier in 1979. But you didn't come here to hear me cry in my beer."

Truer words were never spoken, Frank.

"We came, in fact, seeking background information on the Bainbridge family," Mac enlightened him. "You are the natural depository of such, including that which has not had occasion to find its way into print or public gossip."

Frank's eyes narrowed and he took his feet off the desk, regarding Mac with a look that reminded me he had once been a journalist before he became a gladhander.

"So that's the way it is!" he said. "You're on the Ophelia Bainbridge murder case."

"Possibly," Mac jousted.

"Come on, Frank," I said. "Spill. We're starting at ground level here, just up from the basement."

He eased back into the chair, which I noticed was as well-padded as he was. "Okay. Well, you know they're old money—so old most people don't know where it started. Fact is, the Bainbridge fortune initially came from river transportation. The original Ezra Bainbridge back in the early nineteenth century ran a barge business that one of his descendants sold for millions to some East Coast outfit back in the 1920s, when that was real money. That was Micah Bainbridge, I think. Fortunately for him and his descendants, he had all that money in land and a car dealership when the stock market crashed in '29. He sold some of the land to buy stocks at pennies on the dollar. The Bainbridges have been the cream of what passes for Erin society ever since."

"Could we, maybe move ahead to this century?" I prodded.

He nodded. "Today's Ezra Bainbridge, the current head of the clan, is best known for not being well known. He keeps a low profile, likes to pull strings from behind the scenes except for his service on a number of boards. But he's shrewder than he looks. I understand he actively manages a large portfolio of stocks with Gulliver Mackie as his advisor."

"Which makes me wonder how he stayed unmarried so long after his first wife died," I said. "Call me cynical."

"Okay, Cynical. Maybe he just didn't find the right woman until Fleur came along." He paused. "If you're thinking she's a gold-digger, that there's anything to those abuse allegations that are floating around, you can unthink it. Most people don't know she has a pile of her own from operating a hugely successful online vintage clothing business. Google 'Classic & Classy.' That's the name of the company, which she sold a few years ago for a tidy sum, but

Fleur's classy too. Rory Campbell, her first husband, had a good one there and he blew it with his gambling and drinking. At least, that's what it looks like from the outside. But I shouldn't talk about other people's marriages."

Why stop now, Frank? The comment made me wonder for a fleeting moment whether a less than harmonious situation in the Woodford abode is what kept Frank coming into the office every day even though at his age he could have stayed home and collected Social Security years ago.

"And Ezra's children?" Mac prodded, dragging my thoughts back to the pesky business of Ophelia's murder.

"Let's start with the fun one, Des. She was always a rebel with a cause, although the causes keep changing. Right now, it's art. When she was still a teenager, she got a tattoo, married a rocker in a garage band—at least, I think they were married—and had a daughter she named Marigold after the tattoo. Now she's semi-respectable, but what goes around comes around. Daughter Goldie rebelled by getting a business degree at Columbia and staying in New York until COVID brought her back home. Now she works at the Bridges Law Firm as their CPA or some such. You can't get much more establishment than Bridges in this town. Goldie'd be a nice catch for somebody if she wants to get caught."

"And Portia?"

"Poor Portia." He shook his head. "She's a social climber who's run out of ladder. Her ambitions are outsized for Erin."

"She is married, is she not?" Mac asked, knowing full well the answer.

"Right. Right. To her cousin, Arlo Bainbridge."

"Her cousin!" That was me.

"Second cousin, to be exact. Ezra and Arlo's late father, Randolph, were first cousins, grandsons of Noah Bainbridge, Jr." I had a flashback to the tour Lynda and I took of Fallingwater, Frank Lloyd Wright's late-in-life architectural masterpiece in southwestern Pennsylvania. The original owners of the home, Mr. and Mrs. Edgar J. Kaufmann, of the old Pittsburgh department store family, were first cousins.

"I always had the impression they married to keep the money in the family," Frank gossiped on. "And they have plenty of that, of course. Arlo collects vintage cars— Duesenbergs, Auburns, Pierce-Arrows, and such. There was a joke going around that he thought his wife's first name was 'Porsche' until their honeymoon. I hear he dabbles in a little day trading, too."

"That only leaves the late, much-lamented Ophelia in your survey of the immediate family," Mac said.

Frank Woodford shrugged. "You must have known her better than I did, but I'd say she was a lot like her—"

"Hi, guys!" Johanna Rawls, who always reminded me of one of those Nordic types I see in ads for Gate 1 Travel tours of Scandinavia, stood in the open doorway of Frank's office. She had a reporter's notebook in hand. "Don't let me interrupt."

"You already did," Frank said. But he didn't sound peeved, nor should he have. What's the use of being a journalist if you can't stick your nose—in this case, a cute one—into other people's business? And Tall Rawls, Lynda's protégé and number two fan behind yours truly, is quite a journalist. She's so good I keep wondering how long Erin's little paper can keep her.

"Sorry," Johanna tossed off, not trying to sound like she meant it. "Chewing over the Bainbridge murder, are you? I wanted to talk to you about that, Mac."

He bowed. "I would be happy to oblige, to the extent that I can, trusting your discretion where necessary." *Got that?*

"Take it into the newsroom, will you?" Frank said. He made a shooing motion with his hand. "I have work to do." *Translation: "I have a tee time with an advertiser."*

We dutifully deserted the head honcho's office for the newsroom, which was a conglomeration of computers, desks, mismatched chairs, and paperwork just like every newsroom I've ever entered regardless of the paper's size. The small staff of employees and freelancers had cubicles but spilled out of them. Ben Silverstein, Johanna's immediate boss with the title of news editor, looked like he was struggling with some elusive word choice as he stared at his screen in the other end of the newsroom.

"So," Johanna said, "have you solved it yet?"

"Surely you jest!" Mac said. No doubt he wanted to add something like, *"Even I, McCabe the Magnificent, Master of All Mysteries, am not that good."* But he settled for: "I want to say for the record that Chief Hummel has not asked for my help in this matter and that I have complete confidence in the ability of the Chief and his team to solve the slaying of my much-respected colleague, Professor Ophelia Bainbridge."

Johanna didn't write. "So noted, Mac. Now, dish."

He tried to look reluctant but didn't quite manage it. "If I were to say to you that I find Oscar's conviction that Ophelia's death was the by-product of a botched robbery wholly unconvincing, and you reported my skepticism online and in print, two consequences would ensue: Oscar would be annoyed to a degree that would put serious strains on our friendship, and the killer would be put on the alert."

"So, of course, you're not saying that." She put down her notebook and shot Mac an *"Are you kidding me?"* look. "You don't seriously think you can sniff around this case without word of what you're doing reaching Oscar, the killer, and the ferry boat operator by dinner time, do you?"

"I had my hopes, perhaps unrealistically."

"Excuse me." That was a new voice—a *really* new voice, one that none of us knew—and we all looked in that direction to see to whom it belonged.

He was a man in his mid-thirties, a little taller than my six-one, neither slender nor showing evidence of missed meals, with clear blue eyes and dirty-blond hair that was equally shaggy on his head and on his face in the form of a scraggly beard. Lynda later told me he was handsome in a rakish sort of way, and I'll take her word for it as a connoisseur of male attractiveness. He wore khaki slacks and a blue knit polo shirt. But never mind any of that. His right hand was fiddling with a curved pipe as he stood there regarding us rather awkwardly. Shades of Sherlock! Ben Silverstein is about the only person I know who smokes one of those things. "I'm looking for Johanna Rawls," the intruder said.

"Guilty," volunteered that worthy. From the look on her face, I'd say he certainly had her attention.

"Oh, hi! I'm Buck Melonic, from CNS."

He gave her his card. "B.U. Melonic," she read aloud.

"Buckminster Upton, if you want to rub it in, but Buck will do except for the byline and the card."

"I know that name," Johanna said. "You wrote a feature story about Ophelia Bainbridge a while back."

"That's right. I read about her in the *Observer* and thought she was worth a feature."

"And you're back in town to cover her murder?"

"I'm afraid so. I saw your story online this morning and immediately hit the road."

"You'll want to meet these guys."

She introduced us ("Sebastian McCabe, generally called Mac, and Jeff Cody") and we did the handshakes bit, with Melonic showing no lack of enthusiasm in the hand-pumping. "I was going to look you up next," he told Mac. "You're my favorite mystery writer, by the way. I especially loved the locked room mysteries in *Hocus-Pocus* and *Out of Thin Air*. They're like Golden Age mysteries but set right now. And Damon Devlin rocks! Of course, I know that you're a sleuth yourself, which is just amazing."

"So, you've read my books about Mac's cases?" I said.

"Uh, well, not exactly." *How do you "not exactly" read a book?* "But I've followed the podcasts with Lynda Teal."

"Oh. That's my wife," I informed him.

"Really? Excellent!" *I think so.* "I just listened to her *Murder in Lockdown*, the one about that Stuart Diamond case last year."

I prefer the title I put on my account of the case, *No Ghosts Need Apply*, available wherever you bought this book. But Lynda's title is great, too!

Melonic handed Mac and me each one of his cards and stuck the unlit pipe in his mouth as if striking a pose. The cell phone, e-mail address, and Twitter handle were on the back. The front just said:

B.U. MELONIC
Reporter

Central News Service
Wheeling, W.Va.

Erin is about a four-hour trek by car from Wheeling, mostly on I-70.

"Anyway," Melonic said, signaling that he was moving on from the buttering up phase, "the reason I was going to look you up next, Mac, is that I know from Ms. Bainbridge's father that he's asked you to look into her murder."

Mac arched an eyebrow. "How so?"

"I just came from interviewing the old man in his library. What a place! That was one tough conversation, I'm sure I don't have to tell you. Man, he looked slammed. He also seemed to have trouble processing everything, like he was a few steps behind. His wife didn't even want him to talk to me, but he insisted. He wheeled himself to the front door when she was trying to get rid of me. And even though he was a little off, he made sense. He talked about his daughter, and how special she was even though she was part of a set of three, and how he didn't believe the Erin police were up to solving her murder because they bought into the wrong idea from the start. He also said something about 'What ugly sights of death within mine eyes.'"

"That is a quote from Shakespeare's *Richard III*," Mac enlightened him. "Act One, I believe." *Which scene?*[5]

Without reacting to that information, Melonic produced a phone from his pocket, hit the "record" app, and stuck it out toward Mac. "So, tell me, what's your theory about who killed Ophelia Bainbridge?"

"Have you talked to Chief Hummel?" Mac parried.

"I want to get your thoughts. He's next on my list."

"He should have been first."

Melonic shrugged. "Maybe. But I'm here now."

"I have always been available to the press—" Mac began.

"That's true," Johanna inserted. Maybe she wanted to make sure Melonic didn't forget she was there.

"—however, I feel constrained in this instance because Chief Hummel has not asked for my assistance. Therefore, I have nothing further to say. And if I did, I would say it to Johanna exclusively for several reasons."

She's local talent, she gets all the details right (including the spelling of "McCabe"), and she's a good friend.

Tall Rawls tore her eyes away from Melonic long enough to give Mac a grateful look.

Melonic made a major production number out of hitting the "record" app again to turn off that function, then returning the phone to his pocket. "All right, then, let's start over. I don't really see myself in competition with the local press. We can co-operate on this, Ms. Rawls."

"Johanna, please."

I was starting to feel sorry for Johanna's vertically challenged boyfriend, the affable but awkward Seth Miller.

---

[5] Scene 5—*S.McC.*

"Johanna, then. And I'm willing to go off the record with you, Mac. I'm sure you know how that works: I won't print anything I can't get confirmed elsewhere when it comes to any theories that you explore. But knowing what's up as you go along will help Johanna and me to write our stories later when you tie a ribbon on this thing."

"I'm in!" Johanna announced.

It would be painful to describe how Mac let them chase him until he caught them, so I'll pass over that. Within a few minutes the big guy was pontificating from the comfort of a broad chair in the *Observer*'s conference room, although he insisted that Melonic not record it.

"Ophelia Bainbridge died within reach of a yellow columbine flower, as if she were grasping it at her death," he said. The look on her face confirmed that Oscar hadn't shared this tidbit with Johanna. "That fact cannot be without significance. Given her passion for the traditional detective story, a zeal that coincidentally matches my own, I believe that Ophelia was attempting to identify her murderer just as did the victims in hundreds of Golden Age detective stories."

"Awesome!" Johanna exclaimed.

"But what could it mean?" Melonic added.

"That is the question with which I am struggling. Let me not talk in terms of suspects so much as observations." He ticked them off on his right hand. "The shape of the columbine has been compared to an eagle, a dove, or the hat of a jester. That is, to say the least, inconclusive. Ophelia might have indicated any of those, or none of them. Perhaps, in fact, she meant something much more general. She could have simply been saying 'flower,' for example. The name 'Fleur,' as in Ophelia's stepmother Fleur Bainbridge, means 'flower' in French, a language in which Ophelia was fluent. Desdemona Bainbridge has a yellow flower tattooed on her bosom. Portia Bainbridge is said to be the family member most attached to the English garden at Stratford Court, in which flowers abound. There is also a gardener there."

"Wow!" Johanna said. "All those possibilities! But, you know, they all seem like pretty weak connections, if you think about it."

"I merely stated facts."

Mac had moved from the specific (columbine) to the general (flower) too quickly to suit me.

"It is also a fact," I said, "that there is something called the language of flowers, in which different flowers are associated with certain emotions or characteristics. There's a book in Ezra's library all about it—*A Rose by Any Other Name: The Language of Flowers in Shakespeare*."

"So, what does a columbine mean?" Melonic asked.

Mac didn't give me a chance to answer. "Ah, therein lies the rub, the weakness of Jefferson's theory that renders it both unhelpful and unlikely. Columbine has a wide range of meanings. It can signify folly or foolishness, flattery or insincerity, or fortitude. The Greeks and Romans associated it with the goddess of love. With all those meanings, how could Ophelia know that the correct one would be transmitted? That assumes, of course, that she had learned something about the language of flowers in recent weeks."

He recapped our meeting with her in Ezra's library.

The room went quiet for a while. Melonic and Johanna looked at each other, both seeming to enjoy it, then Melonic looked at Mac. "Anything else?"

"What do you expect?" I asked, a little nettled. "The body is barely cold."

"Although Jefferson's statement is inaccurate a day after the murder, his point is quite valid," Mac told the press. "I have barely begun."

"That language of flowers thing may be ambiguous, but there does seem to be a certain Shakespearean theme in this family," Melonic mused. "All three of the triplets have names of characters from the Bard's plays."

Before we could go anywhere with that, Mac's phone erupted. He arched an eyebrow when he saw who was calling.

"Excuse me," he told us. "I think I should answer this call." He did so. "Sebastian McCabe here! I am surprised to hear from you. Well, that is quite kind. You can be sure of my discretion. Indeed! Thank you for calling."

As Mac disconnected, the look on his face said the wheels were turning in the McCabe mind.

"What was that all about?" I asked, saving the scribes in the room the effort.

"A lead," Mac said. "And without a doubt a lead worth pursuing."

"Specifically?" Tall Rawls pressed with a bit of steel in her baby blues.

"On that point, my dear Johanna, I am afraid I must remain coy."

"What the hell!" Melonic exploded.

"When I assured the caller of my discretion, I did not mean I would share the information with two journalists. At least, not at this time."

"When, then?" Johanna said.

"When we investigate that lead and it bears fruit or does not bear fruit."

"When he feels like it," I translated.

Chapter Eight
All That Glisters

"Are you going to at least tell me?" I asked when we were back in Mac's gas-gobbling 1959 Chevy, which is the approximate size and color of a fire engine with tail fins.

"Of course, old boy!" Mac lit up a ruinously expensive Antonio de la Cova cigar and I rolled down the passenger-side window. "The caller was Holly Burdette. Apparently no longer concerned that I am led astray by confirmation bias, she wished to inform me that Ophelia's cell phone showed that she had an appointment with someone at five o'clock on the afternoon of her death. Ms. Burdette more than hinted that she believes this is a stronger clue to the killer than the columbine flower."

"Oscar was too busy to call you himself?"

"I gather that Ms. Burdette was informing me on her own initiative. She said something about enjoying fireworks. That sounded ominous, so when Oscar gets around to telling me I will feign surprise."

"Good idea. But enough of fun and games. Who was Ophelia supposed to meet on the day of the murder?"

"The full name of the individual did not appear on her telephone calendar, just an initial—D."

It's not bragging to say it didn't take long for the penny to drop, given that our suspect list already included—

"Des Bainbridge!"

"That is a certainly a possibility that we should explore by going to her home and asking her," Mac said.

"The direct approach, eh? What if Gibbons or one of Oscar's other officers is there?"

"Surely it is only natural that we would wish to express to Desdemona our sympathy on the loss of her sister?"

Des Bainbridge's house, separated from Ophelia's by a well-maintained lawn, was a Victorian painted lady. It was mostly the same bright shade of violet as the owner's hair, with a yellow trim that reminded me of her tattoo. We only saw the outside because she never answered the bell.

"Maybe the universe is telling us we're on the wrong track," I suggested. "Let's bail."

"Not yet, old boy. Having come this far, we might as well look in on Portia."

The third Bainbridge triplet lived between Des and Ezra in a yellow brick Colonial dwelling, probably about five bedrooms and a library or parlor, with a six-car garage in the rear. But it was her husband-cousin, Arlo Bainbridge, who came to the door with a harassed expression on his face. He was mid-height and mid-40s, wearing a flat cap, a patchwork plaid shirt, and loafers. He didn't look like a guy who could afford to collect classic cars, but that's how those old-money types are.

"Please tell me you're not reporters or cops," he said without preamble.

"Innocent," I quipped. "McCabe and Cody of SBU."

"Oh, yeah. Sure. I know you. You were at the fundraiser a few weeks ago. Sorry. A policeman talked to Portia this morning, then a wire service reporter came looking for her an hour or so ago."

Melonic didn't mention that. He was holding out on us!

"I knew Ophelia well and would like to extend my sympathy to her sisters," Mac said, telling the truth but not the whole truth and nothing but.

"She's working out her grief at The Bull's Eye," Arlo said.

Mac raised an eyebrow.

"That's the shooting range where the women of WASP meet," Arlo added.

"I know it well, for I shoot my Colt .32 there on a regular basis. I find it helpful to the thinking process while I am plotting a novel. We shall pay Portia a visit."

Arlo Bainbridge shook his head. "It's a helluva thing, isn't it? Murdered! That doesn't happen to Bainbridges. And to think we were home watching *Antiques Roadshow* at the time, just a few yards away. That could have been us!"

"There but for the grace of God," Mac said dryly, no doubt as impressed as I was by Arlo's touching response to the death of his sister-in-law.

But Arlo had already moved on mentally. "Who owns the Chevy convertible?"

"I have that good fortune," Mac said.

"Nice wheels."

"What are you thinking?" I asked Mac when said wheels were under us and moving. "Because I can almost hear the gears moving in the McCabe brain. And don't bother with that cigar; it's a short trip to the range."

He sighed. "I was thinking that there were notable features about Mr. Bainbridge's alibi of watching television. The first is that he offered it, rather subtly, without being asked. The second is that it depends on his wife, who is not herself beyond suspicion."

Some of the other small businesses in the strip mall where The Bull's Eye Gun Shop & Shooting Range is located, in the newer part of Erin just outside of downtown, didn't make it through the pandemic. But the range seemed to be doing a brisk business, judging by the cars outside.

In a nice accident of timing, Portia Bainbridge and Ashley Crutcher were just exiting the building when we pulled up in the Macmobile. Ashley is an old friend that Mac had once helped prove innocent of killing her husband.[6] She's 35, brunette, and pleasingly shaped, since you asked. More relevant, presumably, Ashley is a member of WASP and works as a paralegal for Erica Slade, Erin's most prominent defense attorney and ex-spouse of county prosecutor Marvin Slade. (It's complicated.)

"Hello, strangers!" Ashley hailed.

"It does seem as though it has been a long time since we have encountered each other, Ashley—far too long," Mac said, proving that he can turn on the bonhomie when he wants to. "Mrs. Bainbridge"—he turned to her—"it would be fatuous of me to imply that my grief at the death of your sister can match your own. However, she was a friend and colleague and I mourn her loss. You have my deepest sympathies."

---

[6] See "Dogs Don't Make Mistakes" in *Rogues Gallery* (MX Publishing, 2014).

"And that of the entire St. Benignus community she served so well for so long," I chimed in, unoriginally but sincerely.

"Thank you both." That sounded a little rote, but probably she was just drained from the emotion of it all. What would it be like for her to look into the casket at the visitation two or three days hence and see her own face? The thought gave me shivers.

"Sometimes it's not easy working for a firm that defends murderers," Ashley said, "but somebody has to do it. Take care of yourself, Portia. See you later, Mac, Jeff." She scooted off.

"You fear for your own security?" Mac asked Portia.

"What? Oh, the shooting. No, I find it therapeutic. I have to thank Mitzi Gold for that, the unethical louse. She suggested that Ophelia, Des, and I bond over a mutual hobby. Shooting was Ophelia's idea. I guess that's ironic. Didn't do her much good when some asshole broke into her house, did it?"

"There was no break-in."

"Of course there was, McCabe! A burglar killed her. It could have been any of us at Stratford Court."

"Including you, you mean. That is what your husband said when we spoke to him a few minutes ago. He noted that you were home watching television at the apparent time of the murder."

"*He* was watching television," she corrected. "I was reading a novel about ancient Rome. That's what we were doing before and after dinner. Not that it matters what we were doing. Poor Ophelia!"

"Chief Hummel believes that her killer was a burglar, I grant you. However, I beg to differ, if by burglar one means a person unknown to her who entered the home without her permission. The killer either used a key or was admitted by Ophelia."

Looking around and seeing that the strip center was virtually deserted, and certainly no one was close enough to hear him, Mac laid it all out for her: the lack of forced entry, the valuable items left untouched. But he skipped the part about Ophelia's scheduled appointment on the afternoon of her death with a person signified by the initial D.

"You're saying my sister was murdered by someone she knew?" If Portia was faking shock, she was good at it. But maybe she had practice. "There were times I wanted to wring her neck, but that was just sister stuff. Who could possibly want to hurt Ophelia?"

Mac answered obliquely. "Did she have a romantic partner?" The question already had been asked and answered, but not by Portia.

She shook her head. "No. Not since her husband died. At least, I don't think so. I guess she didn't tell Des and me everything. We've had our problems. You know that. The whole damned town knows that, thanks to Mitzi Gold." *And the publicity created by your lawsuit against her!* "But still, we were all sisters. More than that, we spent nine months in the womb together."

"You and Desdemona have differed with Ophelia recently about your stepmother's treatment of your father," Mac stated.

"Ophelia couldn't see what was right in front of her face. What about it? What does that have to do with anything?"

Mac shrugged his massive shoulders. "Most likely nothing. I bring it up because Ophelia asked me to visit your father and make an assessment of his care based on my observation. That has made me curious about the entire situation. Curiosity may be fatal to felines, but it is essential to investigators."

"'Make an assessment?'" she echoed. "I assumed your degree was in literature, not medicine."

"Assumptions can be hazardous, although in this case you are quite correct. Ophelia called on me as a disinterested third party whose skills in observation have been honed by my experience looking into crimes now and then, with some success. She wanted my opinion."

"Well, now that my poor sister is gone, your opinion is no longer needed. Des and I know what we know: My stepmother either deliberately caused my father to get COVID, or was responsible through neglect, because she only married him for his money. She's still in love with her ex-husband."

"That brings up an interesting point: How did you get the old love letters her former spouse wrote to Mrs. Bainbridge and which she retained?"

That was intended as a gotcha, and it got her.

"How did you—Ophelia told you that?" I had the strong impression that only Ophelia's demise stopped Des from threating to kill her sister. Instead, she said: "I really find it distasteful that she chose to share our family business. I also find it incredible that she didn't see those letters as the proof they are."

"Again, I wonder how you came by them," Mac said mildly.

"Keep wondering."

"Perhaps your other sister, or your niece, or the gardener . . ."

"Is that how you work? Random guesses?"

"Well, no matter," Mac said. "I salute your enterprise. Unless, of course, the letters merely fell in your lap."

"Hardly! I saw through Fleur before she married my father years ago. His getting COVID only convinced me that she got tired of waiting for him to die, probably because she was getting it on with somebody. I knew there must be evidence."

"And how did you get it?"

Discretion vied with pride, and the urge to brag won out. Portia's face was pretty, but at that moment the look on it was not. "I bribed the help, a girl named Nicole Anderson, to let me have a look around one afternoon when Dad and Fleur were playing bridge at the country club. Sweet kid, Nicole. A 21-year-old single mom barely holding things together. I knew she could use some cash. To tell you the truth, I didn't know what I was looking for, but I knew it when I found it."

Mac had his answer, but to me it seemed like we were going down a rabbit hole with no rear exit. Unless, of course, Ophelia pursued the same question as Mac, which led to an argument that ended fatally when Portia picked up a heavy bookend and . . .

"And you kept the letters?" Mac asked, dragging me back to reality.

"I photocopied them for future use and had Nicole return them. She was well-paid for it, too. Are we done here?"

"Not quite," Mac said. "Have the police told you about the circumstances of your sister's death?"

"Just that she was struck with a bookend." Portia paused. "I know the ones. She loved those bookends." It would be too much to say that she choked up, but there was some emotion there.

"There was also a flower near her hand, a yellow columbine," Mac told her. "I believe that could be a message she left to tell us the identity of her killer."

"What? That's nuts."

"Possibly. However, indulge me for a moment. If my premise is correct, what might she be indicating with a flower, or with that particular flower?"

She shook her head. "I have no idea."

"I thought you might have a suggestion because we understand that you are much attached to the garden at Stratford Court."

"I am, but we all grew up with that garden. Ophelia loved columbines. They're mentioned in Shakespeare, aren't they? Dad mentioned that once. She had some in a vase the last time I visited her."

"When was that?"

The day she died, maybe?

"Monday, I think."

That would be the day before the murder.

"Des has a flower tattooed on her chest," I pointed out. "Not a columbine, but a flower."

Portia gave a Mona Lisa smile. "Tattoos on women were just starting to become trendy among the lower classes at the time, which is why she did it. It's a marigold, like her daughter."

"Goldie for short."

"That's right. And she is pure gold, that girl. Everybody loves her, especially her aunts and her grandfather."

Maybe so, but her full name is a flower.

"She was close to Ophelia?" Mac asked.

"Quite. Having no children of her own, Ophelia was free to be very active in helping Des to raise Goldie."

"No father?"

"Everybody has a father, even if it's just a sperm donor." She sighed. "Des has always had a penchant for artistic types. I rather doubt her relationship with that Gamaliel Taylor person is as entirely spiritual as she claims, even though he's old enough to be her father. When she was eighteen, she got pregnant by the drummer in a garage band and made a trip with him to City Hall to get married. Our father eventually made her see the wisdom of getting an annulment. I imagine the romance of living with a rocker faded after Dad cut off her allowance and she had trouble coming up with diaper money. And yet, I think Dad has grown rather fond of the man."

"Goldie's father, you mean?" I asked. "He's still around?"

"He couldn't get much closer. He's the gardener at Stratford Court—Lucius Snedeker."

Chapter Nine
A Man More Sinned Against

"The gardener!" I said as we climbed back into Mac's chariot. "Now he has multiple motives!"

Mac paused from adjusting his seatbelt to cock an eyebrow. "How so?"

"It's obvious! Not only does he work with flowers as his day job, he's also closely associated with both of the sisters that Ophelia was at odds with over their stepmother."

"You refer, of course, to the fact that Mr. Snedeker was once married to Desdemona and has been observed to spend significant time with Portia as she pursues her passion for flowers."

"And maybe that's not the only passion she's pursuing," I snickered.

"I'm not really a full-time gardener," Lucius Snedeker told us, "but it sounds better than 'general dogsbody.' And the garden does take up a lot of my time in spring, summer, and fall. Henry James said, 'a good garden is an organized revel,' and it's my job to organize it. That and anything else the Bainbridge clan want me to do three days a week. I have other clients the other days. Clients, not employers. I'm a free man and I like it that way."

Snedeker, pushing 50 now, must have been in his early twenties when he rushed Des off to the courthouse. He had unkempt dark hair, an easy smile on an outdoor face, and a loping walk. We caught up with him near the gurgling bronze fountain.

"That must be kind of strange," I said, "being a general handyman-cum-gardener for a family you were once part of."

He chuckled as he trimmed a hedge with a big pair of clippers. "I was never part of the family. When Des and I hooked up, I was the lead singer in a band called Howl and waited tables at Doyle's Irish Pub. Into sex, drugs, and rock 'n roll back then—not exactly fit for the Bainbridge bloodline, was I? Not like Arlo Bainbridge, with the same family pedigree and a penchant for collecting cars instead of DUIs. Fortunately for them, there was a slight irregularity in our marriage that made it easy for old Ezra to get it annulled under both civil and church law."

"Would you care to define 'slight'?" Mac said.

"I wasn't divorced from my first wife at the time. I only escaped a bigamy charge under Ohio law because I hadn't seen her for six years and I thought she was dead. Don't look at me like that! I never said I'm perfect."

"None of us is, sadly. Well, you seem to have achieved a sort of *rapprochement* with the Bainbridges."

"They did with me, more like. I think I was more sinned against than sinning, the way they acted like I didn't exist for years. Funny, isn't it? I'm good enough to be on the grounds now, just not in the family tree. That's okay by me. The gig suits, and I'm glad to have it. Ezra Bainbridge was born about 450 years too late, but he's not such a bad guy.

He didn't take much persuading when I asked him to hire me about a dozen years ago so I could be near Goldie. Maybe I'm not the model dad, but I am her father even though her last name is Bainbridge. Des wasn't too keen at first about me being around, but she's used to it now. I don't see her as much as I see Portia, though. As for Ophelia, she was always decent to me, the poor woman, even when I was her sister's bad boy. She didn't marry well either. Kind of runs in the family."

"Had she a paramour of late?" Mac asked.

"A boyfriend? I wouldn't know. My guess is that if she did, she'd keep it on the down low. Dating is hard for a woman her age, and talking about it probably doesn't make it any easier."

This dive into the weeds of romantic relationships made me wonder about Snedeker's current fiddling in that line, if any.

"You must spend a lot of time with Portia here in the garden," I said to him, trying without success not to leer.

"Strictly business," Snedeker assured us. "I'm just the hired help, good for digging up and planting flowers. Snooty Portia wouldn't trust me with anything really important, like walking her dog."

Maybe that's a good thing. Lady Gaga's dogwalker got shot during a dognapping.

"Are you quite certain you have no idea what message Ophelia intended to send with the columbine?" Mac asked. He was circling back to the question that began our conversation when we returned to Stratford Court.

That evoked a vigorous headshake. "I think your whole idea about that is kind of goofy, frankly. A dying message? Come on! Alternative theory? Who am I to have a theory? Okay, maybe the killer threw the flowers on the floor near her body in a fit of pique. Look, just because you've had some luck solving clever murders, that shouldn't cause you to think this is anything different than what the cops say it is—a bungled burglary." *That would be confirmation bias.*

"It is obvious that you are a keen observer of the Bainbridge family dynamics," Mac said, ignoring Snedeker's advice and laying on some soap. "What do you make of the sisters' varying viewpoints about their stepmother?"

"First of all, Fleur isn't a money-grubber, and she hasn't neglected Ezra. The truth is just the opposite—she's been really good for the old man, gave him a new lease on life. Maybe that's what pisses Portia off. It's her show, you know, this bogus accusation. Des is backing her up because she got something out of Portia in return—quid pro quo, don't they call it?"

"What was the quid for her quo?" I asked.

"I have no idea, but I'll tell you this: She couldn't bully or bribe Ophelia."

"And now Ophelia's dead."

My simple statement of fact produced a look of shock on the weathered face of Lucius Snedeker. "What are you saying, Cody?"

"Just an observation."

"Observe it again and I'll knock your block off. Like I said, Ophelia's murder was a bungled burglary by somebody she didn't know—maybe the guy I saw hanging around outside her house the day she was murdered."

Chapter Ten
Strange Bedfellows

This, I know from Lynda, is what they call in the newspaper business "burying the lead"—the failure to put the most important part up top.

"What!"

That was my reaction to Snedeker's tossed-off bombshell. Mac just lifted an eyebrow. I sought clarification:

"You saw a stranger that day?"

The general dogsbody nodded. "I'd never seen him before, so, yeah, he was a stranger to me. A mousey guy in his fifties, balding, thick glasses."

"When?"

"About four-thirty, five o'clock. I wasn't looking at my watch. But it was late afternoon."

"I assume you informed law enforcement?" Mac said, but it was really a question.

"Right. I told the cop who was around here asking questions this morning, name of Gibbons."

Was that only this morning? It had been a long day of poking around, starting early and now ending in the afternoon at Stratford Court, with stops at Oscar's office, the *Observer*, and The Bull's Eye along the way.

"Well," Mac mused, "I am sure that friend Oscar will take that as support for his burglar theory."

"But you're not buying it," I said.

"Of course not, old boy."

"How do you think the guy you saw would have gotten into the house?" I asked Snedeker.

He shook his head sadly. "I told Ophelia not to leave her key under the flowerpot. What a cliché!"

On our way back to Mac's car, I said, "I'm sure you noticed that our gardener friend admits to being on the scene around the time of the murder, and that his story of some mysterious visitor takes attention from him. He could have made it up."

"Certainly! That is undeniable. And what motive do you hypothesize for Mr. Snedeker to kill Ophelia? We have found no confirmation of your suggestion that he acted on behalf of the remaining sisters. He does not appear to be particularly close to either of them, nor is it likely that 'hired killer' comes under his duties."

"We only have his word for the state of his relationships with Des and Portia," I pointed out.

"Granted. Is there any other theoretical motive that you can adduce for Mr. Snedeker?"

I thought fast. "Maybe he 'attempted familiarities' with Ophelia, as you might put it, and she strongly objected. Or maybe he was dipping into the till somehow."

"Neither of those conjectures is totally implausible," Mac admitted. "Let us put that to one side for further consideration while we interview other members of the Bainbridge brood."

It's a good thing I have a trusty assistant to keep my office humming, a mobile by which I can be reached wherever I am, and a boss's boss (initials GK) who had already given his thumbs up to Mac—and by extension me—investigating the murder of Ophelia Bainbridge. Because the next morning, Thursday, found Mac and me at Desdemona's painted lady home, this time with the owner in residence.

Des is something of a painted lady herself, with her violet hair and a heavy eye shadow to match, not to mention the tattoo. She answered the door with a lit cigarette in her hand. Home is one of the few places where a person can still smoke (if one's cohabitant allows it, which Kathleen Cody McCabe does not).

Mac hit her with some blather about being there to offer sympathy. This was not completely implausible, given that Des and Kate moved in the same art circles and occasionally caught up at lunch.

"Come on in," she said.

Des led us into a spacious living room, decorated with large paintings and a profusion of sculptural pieces on the fireplace mantle and the end tables. Later, I wished I'd paid more attention to that. In the moment, the Cody brain was taking note of the other two occupants of the room: Gamaliel Taylor and Goldie Bainbridge.

"Ah, Erin's answer to Nancy Drew," Taylor said, extending his hand to Mac. *He's actually more like Nero Wolfe, at least in size.* "I've been hearing about you since I came to town. You really have had remarkable luck as an amateur sleuth."

Mac shook his hand, showing remarkable restraint in the face of a comment that managed to be simultaneously simpering and insulting. "Let us say good fortune rather than luck," he said. The difference was that Sebastian McCabe makes his own good fortune by dint of brainwork, a vast mental database of diverse knowledge, and persistence. But I'm not sure Taylor caught that.

I shook Taylor's hand, too, but I wanted to wash mine afterward. I couldn't get past the idea that he was an aging Lothario, carefully adopting the unshaved and unshorn look despite the graying of his fair hair. Portia hadn't exaggerated when she said he was old enough to be Des's father. He stood close to her, although I noticed that he kept his hands to himself. It seemed to me that he looked . . . sad. Could it be that he really was moved by Ophelia's demise? Or was he sucking up to his patron?

Mac turned his attention to Goldie. She sat on a love seat stroking an orange tabby cat, somehow looking smaller and younger than when we'd seen her the day before.

"It is good that you have taken some time off from work to take care of yourself after the traumatic experience of finding the body," Mac assured her.

"Actually, I took time off to take care of my mother. I'm going to stay here for a few days."

She shot Des a look that I couldn't read, but I was pretty sure that neither her mother nor Gamaliel Taylor thought Goldie's help was needed.

"Isn't that your aunt's?" I asked the young woman, nodding toward the feline. I was trying to cheer her up. The only thing cat lovers love more than cats and posting pictures of cats is talking about cats.

She nodded. "He let her think so. She called him Eliot, like the poet. I guess I'm his now, an inheritance from Aunt Ophelia."

I had a flashback to Lynda and me taking care of the late Maggie Barton's Binkie and Bunkie until Triple M let them move in with her. As far as I can tell, cat "ownership" involves responsibilities but no rights. Hardly a motive for Goldie to assist her aunt from this vale of tears. The money she inherited was another matter, at least in my book. A woman Ophelia's age from one of Erin's wealthiest families, with no kids and a simple lifestyle, must have had scads of it tucked away.

"You're not just paying a sympathy call," Des told Mac. She gave the coffin nail a good drag, then blew the smoke toward the ceiling. Lynda used to do that before she broke the habit. "Do you want our alibis?"

"It wouldn't hurt," I said. "You know, just for the record."

"I was joking!"

"I got home from work at five-thirty and cooked dinner," Goldie said. "I like to cook. Gamaliel stopped by to eat with us."

"Until then, I spent the afternoon in my travel camper working on some notes for a lecture," he lectured. "As you know, I am the artist-in-residence under a program established and partly funded by Desdemona with community support, for which I am most grateful."

"I had a meeting at the Shinkle with Adam that went until about five-thirty," Des said. "Satisfied?"

Mac didn't quite answer. "Then you did not have an appointment with Ophelia?"

"Certainly not." She blew smoke. I felt grateful that she continued to aim it above our heads, but even at that the clouds were getting thick in there. "If this is about that initial D in the calendar on Ophelia's phone, I can assure you that my sister and I didn't need to make appointments to meet or talk to each other."

Sebastian McCabe never sputters, but it was a near thing. "May I ask how you knew—"

"I had a call from a policeman named Gibbons."

"I see. Well, I should have known that Colonel Gibbons would not have let that stone go unturned despite the Chief's burglar theory. And rightly so. No doubt by now he is pursuing another prospect in the form of a visitor to your sister's home that afternoon."

Des frowned. "What visitor?"

"Perhaps 'visitor' is an inexact or even inaccurate nomenclature. Your former husband observed a man, quote, 'hanging around' outside Ophelia's home. Is Mr. Snedeker a reliable observer?"

After a meditative puff she admitted, "Lucius doesn't hallucinate, so far as I know."

"How close are you two?" I asked.

"Not very," Goldie asserted. I took that as definitive.

"Mr. Snedeker described the individual as in his fifties, balding, with thick glasses, not robust in physique." This last was Mac-speak for "mousey." "Does that sound familiar to you?"

She shook her head. "Not off-hand."

"Is it possible that he was a gentleman caller?"

That earned a laugh. "I'm pretty sure Ophelia swore off men after the disaster that was Devan O'Rourke."

"She didn't, though," Goldie spoke up. "Or if she did, she swore off swearing it off."

Her mother turned on her. "What?"

"Aunt Ophelia was experimenting with a dating app," Goldie said. "She told me."

"That's absurd!" Des said.

"It's true."

Taylor put a comforting hand on Des's shoulder. "My dear," he muttered.

"I had no idea." Des bent down to stub out her cigarette in a blown-glass ashtray. That looked odd because Taylor kept his hand on her shoulder while she bent, and he was even taller than the Bainbridge girls.

Goldie looked embarrassed. "Maybe you didn't know her as well as I did," she told Des, "even after relationship therapy. Aunt Ophelia told me things, but that's all I know about that. She didn't tell me whether she had a prospect."

Dead end. Time to regroup.

"Ophelia died with a columbine flower near her hand, as if she had been holding it," Mac pointed out. By now, everybody in town knew that; it was the focus of Johanna's second-day story that morning about the murder, which duly quoted Oscar doubting the flower's significance. Tall Rawls had taken the off-the-record tip from Mac and run with it. "Did that particular floral variety hold some special meaning to her that you know of?"

While Des hugged her arms and stared blankly, her daughter said, "She changed out the flowers in that vase every now and then. When whatever was in there died, she substituted new ones. The columbine had been there several days, I think. Why do you ask?"

"Because she may have been trying to tell us by means of that flower the identity of her killer," Mac said.

Taylor gave a laugh that was about as natural as Des's violet hair. "That sort of thing doesn't happen in real life. With all due respect, McCabe"—people only say that when they mean no respect is due—"perhaps you should leave this one to the professionals."

"On the one hand," I told Mac after escaping the cigarette-poisoned atmosphere of Des's house, "Des and her aging boy toy seem like strange bedfellows. He isn't exactly old money. On the other hand, he seems to live the bohemian lifestyle that she aspired to way back when she married Goldie's father."

"I am not certain that they are bedfellows at all, old boy. I saw no evidence that Mr. Taylor is living there, and I detected no sexual vibrations between the two. His interest seemed fatherly."

"Since when did you become an expert on the subject of sexual vibes?"

Mac ignored the question and moved on. "Kate is of the expert opinion that Mr. Taylor gets through life more by charm than by talent."

We settled into Mac's car.

"I don't even find him charming," I said. "He exudes more oil than one of Lynda's Italian salads. Do you believe Des's denial that she's the 'D' on her sister's calendar?"

"I find it credible. Her point that one need not tightly schedule a meeting with a sibling who is also a near neighbor is a valid one, although we had to ask."

"So that leaves The Mysterious Stranger."

"For the nonce, yes. There is the intriguing possibility that he is—"

Mac's phone erupted just as he reached for his keys to start the engine. He pulled it out of his pocket and put it on speakerphone in one smooth move. "Hello, Johanna."

"Hi, Mac. Hi, Jeff, if he's there."

"I'm here." *Where else would I be? In my office? LOL!*

"I was just calling to see, you know, whether you came up with anything. Off the record. Or even better, something I can use."

"I am afraid that would be premature," Mac said, "even on an off-the-record basis."

"But you are working at it, right?"

"Off-the-record, yes. The status is quo, one might say."

"That doesn't help much. Have you run into that cute reporter?"

"We have not, although we found traces yesterday that he was ahead of us."

"Oh. Well, I was just curious. Keeping up with the competition, you know."

You were never that curious about Morrie Kindle of the AP, who is not cute.

"Might I inquire what Oscar has told you today?"

"You might inquire, and I might answer." *Nice wordplay!* "He said, 'The investigation is ongoing, and we have two substantial leads involving a person of interest.' Same old, same old. That's why I was hoping you could tell me more."

Mac looked happier than he should have that Oscar apparently had nothing more than The Mysterious Stranger and Ophelia's appointment with D. That added up to two, and we knew that Oscar had both. So those were his two leads.

"I look forward to sharing more with you when I can," Mac told Tall Rawls.

"Make it soon, will you?"

Mac assured her that was his most earnest wish, and they disconnected.

"You have the nicest way of saying 'We have no clue,'" I told Mac.

"We most certainly do have a clue, Jefferson. The challenge is discerning what it means."

"Ophelia's relationship with her husband sounds like my parents," Lynda said after the Cody offspring were in bed and so were we. "Lots of passion in the relationship, both negative and positive."

I'd given my admirable spouse a complete rundown of the long day, including that encounter with Serena Mason outside the *Observer*. Lynda wondered what she'd been up to, which made two of us. Now we'd circled back to discussing the murder victim.

"I had the same thought about your parents," I said, "but let's not talk about them." Lynda's mother is an Italian supermodel and her father is a retired Army colonel with mysterious attachments to military intelligence. I'm not sure which one scares me more. When the two of them are together, which isn't often, anything can happen from throwing things to advanced PDAs.[7] They produced Lynda's younger sister, Chicago-area university librarian Emma Teal, several years after their divorce.

"It's sad that Ophelia's husband died so horribly."

I sat up in bed. "What if he didn't?"

"What do you mean, 'what if he didn't'?"

"I mean, what if he didn't? What if he's still alive and of a murderous disposition after years of hiding from Ophelia

---

[7] For harrowing details, see the account of our wedding in *The* 1895 *Murder* (MX Publishing, 2012).

and everything she represented to him—the old money, the privilege." The idea sounded even better out loud.

"How can he still be alive?" Lynda wanted to know. The answer was easy:

"He supposedly died in a whitewater rafting accident in Brookville, Indiana, about a dozen years ago. Maybe they never found the body. There would be nothing suspicious about that. Bodies get lost in rivers all the time. He could have faked his own death. It's happened before in Erin."

"Wait a minute." Lynda looked thoughtful. And distractingly beautiful, despite her slightly crooked nose! "If it happened before, wouldn't that reduce the chances that it happened again?"

"Only in fiction. I read a news story earlier this year about a man who died of cancer at age 32, according to an announcement from his wife. But later, somebody tried to replace the photo in his Wikipedia entry with a photo of someone else—using an account created by the supposedly dead guy. And, get this: said guy was under fraud investigation by the FBI when he" —air quotes—"died."

"Well," Lynda said with a yawn, "you might be on to something, but I think the idea is creepy. Can we talk about something else, *tesoro mio?*"

I moved her way. "We don't have to talk at all, my sweet."

Chapter Eleven
Toil and Trouble

"TGIF," Popcorn said in my office the next morning, handing me a mug of decaf joe.

I stopped my computer research of the allegedly-dead-but-not Nicholas Alahverdian, a story which had more twists and turns than a mountain highway. (And even more since that day. Google the name and see.) She settled in.

"So, what have you boys been up to that I promise not to tell Oscar about, Scout's honor?"

"You were a Scout?"

"Heck, yeah—Girl Scout First Class. It's like what an Eagle Scout is for guys."

A sore point, that: I didn't make it to Eagle Scout; Mac did.

"Okay, then," I said, "do you want it in chronological order or bottom line first?"

"Bottomline me on it. What have you got?"

"Nothing to text home about. We talked to Ophelia's sisters, her niece, her brother-in-law, the gardener—who is also Goldie's father, by the way—and the Shinkle's artist-in-residence who is hovering around Des like bees around a flower. At this point, they all seem to have fairly porous alibis but also no really strong motives. I just don't buy the idea that she was a great danger to Portia's campaign against Fleur.

Probably the strongest motive is Goldie, who inherits her aunt's money and has already been acquired by her cat."

Popcorn looked skeptical, for which I didn't blame her. "What does Mac think?"

Why does everybody care what Mac—

"He's stuck on the idea that Ophelia left a clue to her killer in the form of the flower by her body," I replied. "That could point back to Goldie, whose name is Marigold, which is a yellow flower. Also, she found the body. And in real life, the person who finds the body most often also created the body in the sense of being the killer. And I can tell from your body language that you aren't buying that, are you?"

"Not for a minute. Goldie's a sweet kid—went to high school with my daughter Bonnie."

"All right, then, here's another idea. What if Ophelia's husband—"

My office phone rang. Grant Kingsley was on the other end, summoning me up to his presidential office on the fifth floor, up one from mine in the Gamble Building. You don't need a deep dive into what followed unless you are reading this at night and in serious need of a soporific. Not that it was an unimportant confab. On the contrary, I knew it was big stuff because my immediate boss, Lesley Saylor-Mackie, was already there on the office couch when GK's executive assistant nodded me in. Saylor-Mackie looked grim. The president himself sat behind his huge power desk, with a painting of Air Force jets flying in formation behind him. The sign on his desk says **LEADERS LEAD**.

"Big challenges require big responses," he began even before I sat down. I made a mental note to work that into a speech for him sometime. "And we have big challenges at SBU these days, like all small colleges and universities.

Revenues are off by fifteen percent since we got slammed by COVID. I wanted to keep you in the loop on our planned course of action to deal with that, Jeff."

He rolled out a lot of numbers before getting to the bottom line, which was that he proposed to lay off professors and curb tenure.

"The faculty will be up in arms, of course," Saylor-Mackie said. "That's going to get sticky."

"But it's the right thing to do," GK said. "Lesley and I are agreed on that."

"Won't the faculty say that revenues are off because we cut tuition in the spring semester?" Anticipating tough questions, and preparing the answers, is part of my job.

"Probably," GK concurred, "but it's not true. The fact is that revenues would have been even less without the tuition reduction because we would have had fewer students. Where the cut hurt us was on the bottom line, but that's temporary. I'm convinced it will pay off in the long run because it helped us keep a high percentage of our students. That's why a lot of colleges and universities, including some big ones, made the same move.

"Anyway, that's in our rearview mirror now and I'm looking ahead. Lesley and I are going to present our restructuring plan to the board of trustees at their quarterly meeting next month. It's a natural follow to pulling back on low-value Ph.D. programs. But even as a former board chair, I'm not sure how the trustees are going to react. We'll need every vote. Which brings me to Ezra Bainbridge. Have you seen him since the murder?"

"I have. It was painful. He wasn't doing so hot *before* the murder, and much worse now."

"I've heard the rumors. Sorry I couldn't be at that bash for the Shinkle the other week. We were at our place in South Carolina." *Life is tough.* "I'll be at Dr. Bainbridge's funeral, of course, although I didn't really know her." He shook his head. "From what I've heard about her, I wish I had. How is Mac coming along with finding the murderer?"

"Believe me, he has no higher priority right now."

Such as teaching, for instance.

After the meeting, instead of walking across campus to Mac's office in Herbert Hall to watch him perform some magic trick, I called him with a verbatim report of my corner-office conversation with GK about the case.

"I shall be at Ophelia's funeral Mass as well," he said.

"Good. We can both look for Devan O'Rourke. His picture is on Wikipedia, if that isn't a phony that he substituted for the real photo."

Mac let me go on at some length while I repeated the whole theory that I'd laid out for Lynda the night before, plus what I'd found on the internet that morning.

"I really must salute your acuity and your industry, Jefferson!" he said.

"You think I'm on to something, then?"

"Alas, no. Your theory, although splendid, lacks the virtue of truth. I had the same notion myself, so I checked. A small story in the *Observer* some weeks later reported that Mr. O'Rourke's body was recovered in the Whitewater River."

"Wrong body," I posited.

"I called Oscar. He checked and assured me that the body, though scarcely recognizable, was identified from dental records."

"The dentist was in cahoots with O'Rourke." I wasn't giving up easily. "O'Rourke probably bribed him."

"Dentists are not known to be an impoverished class, and Dr. Marcum has shown no signs of penury."

I guess not! He's my dentist, and I know what my insurance company shells out to him twice a year.

"On the other hand," Mac droned on, "I am socially acquainted with Dr. Marcum, and he does not exhibit any indications of a significant side income from the false identification of corpses. Nor is there the slightest reason to think that Devan O'Rourke would have sufficient funds to bribe a successful dentist."

Finished beating the dead horse, he stopped.

"All right, maybe it wasn't bribery," I admitted. "Maybe O'Rourke blackmailed him into it."

I could almost hear Mac lift an eyebrow halfway. "Dr. Marcum hardly seems the type to have committed some blackmail-worthy offense."

"Ah-ha! That's exactly what makes an offense blackmail-worthy—the presumed respectability of the blackmail victim."

"Well, this is highly speculative, you must concede." Was that the shuffling of playing cards I heard on Mac's end of the line? "Why would Devan O'Rourke, a little-known poet with no financial resources of his own when he married into the Bainbridge family—I confirmed that with a half-hour of research—want to be believed dead? Although their marriage was by all accounts a stormy one, Ophelia paid to have his poetry published under her own imprint and otherwise provided him with a comfortable life."

I gave a shrug that Mac couldn't see. "Maybe he had a girlfriend and wanted to start a new life in romantic poverty without Ophelia's money. Or maybe he thought that being dead would boost his poetry sales. Who knows? O'Rourke was a poet, and therefore whacko."

Mac didn't deny that. "You get full marks for ingenuity, old boy. When it comes to plausibility, however, your case is sorely lacking." *Since when has that bothered Sebastian McCabe?* "I think we need to look elsewhere for our murderer."

Ophelia's funeral was held the next day, Saturday, at the St. Benignus University chapel, a gem of a church built in federal-style architecture to match most of the original structures on campus. Father Juan Diego Ortega, director of campus ministries, presided.

Lynda and I shared a pew with Mac and Kate. Ezra Bainbridge walked in leaning heavily on a cane and supported by his wife. The remaining Bainbridge sisters filled out the first two pews, along with Arlo, Goldie, and two attractive college-age women I later learned were Arlo and Portia's daughters, Astrid and Harley.

Father Juan directed most of his homily to the Gospel reading, John 14:1-6, about the house of many rooms.

I listened, but I also looked. Call it multi-tasking. David Gunner sat right behind the family. Also present in the chapel were Lucius Snedeker, Serena Mason, Lesley Saylor-Mackie, Grant Kingsley, Gamaliel Taylor and, to my surprise, the CNS reporter B.U. "Buck" Melonic in a pew with the even taller Tall Rawls. I'm just hitting the highlights. The chapel was full, with both town and gown well represented. Grace Langley, SBU board chair, drove in from Chillicothe.

"Did anybody look guilty?" I asked Mac.

"They all did. The living frequently do at funerals."

Chapter Twelve
Rosemary . . . for Remembrance

"How was the funeral, Boss?" Popcorn asked me on Monday morning.

"Sad. Maybe a little sadder than most. How was your weekend? Hot date with Oscar?"

"Hot enough. We went to the Erin Eagles game on Saturday night."

"Spare me the seamy details of minor league baseball. How's he doing with Ophelia's murder?"

"Not ready to go to Mac and cry 'uncle' yet, if that's what you're asking. He figures the man that the gardener saw outside her house on the afternoon of the murder fits perfectly into the burglary scenario."

Oscar had gone public with The Mysterious Stranger in a Tall Rawls story that appeared in Sunday's *Observer*. Her long front-page feature was mostly a rehash with a lot of background about Ophelia, the kind of weekend piece newspapers have rolled out since they were printed on papyrus. But a sidebar included Snedeker's description, via Oscar, of the man outside Ophelia's house on the day of the murder. "We're asking this person to come forward so that we can eliminate him as a suspect," Oscar told Johanna. *Right.*

"Now it's your turn," Popcorn said from behind her coffee mug. "What about Mac?"

"Mac *and* I are collecting and analyzing data and eliminating the impossible so that we can consider the improbable."

"So, you don't have anything either?"

I put on my boss face. "Shouldn't we be working on a news release about Banned Books Week?"

"I have the list of activities right here. Maybe we could get somebody to ban your books. It might help them sell."

We went on our happy way like this through the rest of the day. (See "office wife" in Urban Dictionary. Or "work spouse," if you prefer.) It was after three o'clock when I got a call from Sebastian McCabe.

"New theory?" I said, by way of salutation.

"New body, Jefferson, I regret to report. Portia Bainbridge was found dead in her home this afternoon, bludgeoned. Oscar has decided that our assistance may be of some use after all."

The EMTs were on the scene, Oscar's officers were dusting for fingerprints and taking photos, and Arly Eppensteiner was just leaving as we arrived at the Arlo and Portia Bainbridge residence in Stratford Court. Our coroner, just over five feet of coiled energy, likes to make an appearance at every homicide scene even though Ohio law doesn't require it. I used to think she was a publicity hog, her job being at the mercy of the voters every four years, but I've come to believe she's that *rara avis*, a dedicated public servant.

"No mystery about the cause of death," she told Mac, pushing errant strands of dark, curly hair out of her eyes. "I'm confident the autopsy will show it was blunt force trauma—a carbon copy of what happened to the poor woman's sister."

This time we had no problem getting through the yellow crime scene tape. Lt. Col. L. Jack Gibbons himself signed us in and waved us through in his customary taciturn way.

The inside of the house was what you would expect from the Colonial architecture, filled with well-upholstered chairs and well-polished tables of various heights and sizes. Arlo sat on one end of an overstuffed loveseat, looking lost and alone. His wife's body lay on the floor, covered, but with blood seeping out.

"We are sorry to intrude on you at such a difficult time," Mac told him.

"I knew her all my life," Arlo said, his voice lifeless. "No, I knew her all *her* life. I have to tell Harley and Astrid. How am I going to tell Harley and Astrid? They came home for Ophelia's funeral."

If I were writing the script for the bereaved husband, I would have had him say something about how wonderful Portia was, not the longevity of their relationship. But the bereaved are liable to say anything.

"Maybe you should go somewhere else for a while," Oscar told Arlo. "We need to talk to you some more, but we can do that later."

"I want to stay," Arlo mumbled.

"All right, then. Thanks for coming, Mac. I'd like to get your perspective on this." This was Oscar's way of caving, and we all three knew it. "Mr. Bainbridge here came home from lunch with some friends at the Nonpareil Club in Cincinnati and found Mrs. Bainbridge lying here. He

immediately called 911. She was struck from behind by this."
He held up in his gloved hand a bloodied vase, bronze with
an enameled flower design. "The killer dropped it next to the
body." One of his officers would have taken multiple photos
of the murder weapon where it was found.

"Chinese bronze cloisonne," Mac observed. "That
cannot be inexpensive."

"Three thousand dollars," Arlo said. He struck me as
the kind of guy who would know the price of everything. His
Rolex watch was worth about $4,500, used, unless it was one
of the more expensive models, which it might have been. I
haven't worn my Timex since Mac made it disappear right off
my wrist while he was showing off, but I'm pretty sure it
would show the same time as Arlo's. On the other hand, I
once owned an imitation Rolex—I called it a "Fauxlex"—but
it died after two weeks.

"And then there's this."

Oscar removed the covering over the body to show
that lying near it was what looked to me like some sort of
weed or shrub with a purplish flower.

"By thunder, that is the herb rosemary!" Mac said.

"Whatever," Oscar said. He addressed the newly-
minted widower: "Is that what was in the vase that killed
her?" *Delicately put, Chief.*

Arlo shook his head. "No. Sunflowers. Portia loved
sunflowers. She filled that vase with sunflowers."

"Which are nowhere in evidence," Mac said, just in
case Oscar missed it. "That can scarcely be without meaning.
We are in deep waters, as Sherlock Holmes would say. Surely
you do not posit a second foiled burglary here in Stratford
Court, Oscar?"

Oscar scowled, not in a positing mood, or perhaps not sure what the word meant. "Let's not make any assumptions too fast. Despite what it looks like, the two Bainbridge murders may not be related. This could be the work of a copycat killer."

Mac nodded. "Indeed, it could—copied even to the extent that once again there is no sign of forced entry. On the other hand, perhaps this murder was planned all along, and Ophelia's death was mere camouflage to keep us from considering Portia as the true intended victim."

That kind of thinking always gives me a headache.

Arlo jumped up, out of his daze. "Stop it! Stop it! How can you—" He buried his head in his hands and sobbed. And as he did, it occurred to me that under Ohio law a spouse inherits substantially no matter what the will says; we'd been down that road before. But with both spouses being Bainbridges, this was old money and therefore undoubtedly all tied up in trusts and such designed to keep the money in the family. Estate planning like that would have left Arlo the *cui* of that old "*cui bono?*" question.

"Isn't there somewhere you can go, get away from this for a while?" Oscar asked Arlo.

He unburied his head to say, "Get away? How can I get away? I'll never get away. Portia . . ." He started over. "Des's house, I guess. I could go over to Des's house."

"You would be well advised to do so," Mac advised him.

After a little more cajoling, he did so.

When Arlo was barely out of the room, I asked Oscar: "What do you think the chances are that he did it?"

Oscar shrugged. "Fifty-fifty. I want to listen to the 911 call to see how spazzed out he is when he reports the body, but you can't always tell by that. Being a Bainbridge doesn't deal him out. If there was a reality TV series called *Murders by the Rich and Famous*, it wouldn't run out of material for a damned long time."

Not a bad idea! I made a mental note of it.

"I am unconvinced, albeit persuadable," Mac said.

"Let me just point out to you sleuths that you may call rosemary an herb, but it's still a flower," I said. "In my book, that puts Fleur—as in 'flower'— back on the suspect list. Unless, of course, we can find somebody whose name is Rosemary, which would be even better, although in that case I don't know how the first flower would fit in."

Mac's eyebrows went aloft. "Surely you do not still hold to the theory that the columbine was Ophelia's attempt to name her murderer, old boy?"

It took me a while to process that before I sputtered, "Eh? What do you mean? What other theory is there? You've been carrying the flag for the dying message solution since we got pulled into this!"

"Granted. It now becomes obvious, however, that we have been reading the nature of the message and the identity of its sender all wrong."

"What do you mean 'we'?"

He sailed on as if I hadn't interrupted.

"It is not inconceivable in principle that Portia attempted to identify her killer by grabbing a flower as she lay dying, inspired by her sister's action. If that were the case, however, what happened to the sunflowers that her husband told us were normally in the vase that killed her? They are not in this room." Mac shook his massive head. "No, gentlemen, it is far more likely that the killer left both the rosemary and the columbine to make some sort of statement that is for the moment obscure."

"The killer!" Oscar exploded. "That only makes sense if he's a whack-job. I mean, no sane person goes around leaving a trail of bodies with a calling card attached, even if it's one we can't figure out."

"We will decipher the meaning in due course," Mac said. "We must."

"While you're at it, pull a motive out of your magician's top hat," I suggested. "Never mind the copycat theory and the camouflage theory for a minute and work with the wild idea that the killer actually wanted to kill both Ophelia and Portia. Who would want to do that?"

"Maybe somebody whose initial is 'D,'" Oscar said.

"What do you mean?" Mac deadpanned.

"Don't give me that crapola! As an actor, you make a great detective. I heard Holly call you, and I reamed her good for it. You probably also knew about—"

The ringing of his phone stopped Oscar in mid-fulmination. He checked to see who was calling, then answered.

"Yes, Gibbons. Oh, great." His voice dripped sarcasm. He sighed. "No, I'll go out and talk to her. Thanks."

He disconnected and turned back to us. "It's your pal Rawls. She's outside and wants to talk to me. The press are such ghouls. I guess I'd better get it over with, but not alone. You come with me."

Johanna stood just outside the crime scene tape, chatting with Gibbons, which is pretty much a one-way street. I heard her utter "Aurelia said" before she saw us and opened her notebook.

"Are we looking at a serial killer here, Chief?" she asked by way of hello.

"It's too early to say what we're looking at, Johanna, but serial killers usually attack people who fit a certain profile and aren't related." Not a bad answer, I thought.

She tried again. "Since the women looked a lot alike, is there any chance the killer murdered Ophelia Bainbridge by mistake and came back to rectify the error?"

Great idea! But—

"That's pretty far-fetched, considering that the first Ms. Bainbridge was killed in her own home."

"But do you think the same killer took the lives of both Bainbridge sisters?"

Oscar stuck stubbornly to the facts. "At this point, without going into detail, I can tell you that both women were attacked in their homes and killed in similar ways. Draw your own conclusions."

"I try not to do that, Chief. I'm not a TV reporter."

They both chuckled.

"Do you have any persons of interest?" Johanna asked, now that she had him loosened up.

"You mean in addition to the man reported outside Ophelia Bainbridge's house on the day she died? No."

"Have you had any responses to my story about that man in yesterday's paper?"

"Not yet, but we're still hopeful. Sometimes it takes a while for people to work up the moxie to come forward."

"Were there also flowers at the scene of this crime?" That was a new voice, but a familiar one. Buck Melonic, the

CNS wire service reporter, had snuck up on us. Johanna appeared glad to see him, Oscar considerably less so.

"You're back in town?"

"I didn't have time to leave, Chief. Now, how about my question: Were there also flowers at the scene of this murder?" He held out his phone to record the answer.

"An herb called rosemary, which is like a shrub with flowers—in this case purple—lay near the body."

"What do you think it means?"

"Any answer to that question would be highly speculative at this time."

"So, speculate!" Johanna urged.

Melonic gave her an appreciative look that may have even had something to do with her journalistic skills.

"I don't think I have anything else for you at this time," Oscar said. "I'll let you know when I do." He turned and left.

"But I didn't ask all my questions!" Melonic shouted after him.

"I'll catch you up," Johanna told him. "He deigned to answer a few questions before you got here."

"Thanks, Johanna."

"My pleasure, Buck."

Rent a room, you two!

Melonic lit his curved pipe and looked meditative. "You know, I've always thought I'd make a pretty fair amateur detective myself."

All you need is a deerstalker. You're tall enough. But the attempted blond beard would have to go.

"Indeed." Mac didn't sound thrilled by the comment.

"Yeah. And I've been thinking. I bet it's the murderer who decorated the bodies with flowers, some poor sick soul trying to tell the world why he did it."

"Wow!" Johanna enthused.

"And why did he do so?" Mac asked, waxing skeptical, as if he hadn't proposed the same theory a few minutes earlier.

Melonic gave his shoulders a workout. "I don't know what the flowers mean, but I bet it all goes back to that language of flowers thing we talked about the other day."

Before I could point out that was my hobby horse he'd just mounted, Mac came back with, "That theory does merit reconsideration now that we have two bodies, each with a flower nearby." He fired up a cigar in a sure sign that he was putting the McCabe brain cells through their paces.

"The question, of course, becomes what columbine and rosemary mean taken together," he said. "Or perhaps the presence of both can clarify the meaning of each, which can be ambiguous in the language of flowers."

Melonic removed the pipe from his mouth to ask, "Are both plants in Shakespeare?"

"No doubt you are thinking of Monica Porlock's book. Yes, as a matter of fact—"

And then the hoards descended—a whole pack of noisy journalists from Cincinnati, including the ever-perky Mandy Peters from TV4 Action News and a 12-year-old I didn't recognize from Channel 11 (*Live@11 on TV11!*), as well as Morrie Kindle from the AP and an intern from SBU's own station WIJC-FM. Peters headed right for our little quartet, carrying her own camera as most TV reporters are forced to do these days.

"Ah, the real media have arrived," Melonic said, his voice dripping with derision. Johanna, the audience he was playing to, snickered.

"Hi, Jeff," Peters called. We go way back. I remember when she was a Channel 4 intern as a student at Miami University in Oxford, Ohio, trying to decide whether to change her last name from Petrowski for television. I knew then she had all the right ingredients for a career in TV journalism—lush auburn hair, perfect teeth, a generous mouth, a fine nose, and a voice devoid of accent. She turned out to be a better reporter than most of her counterparts, after a few years at it. "I hope I'm not too late."

"Not at all," I reassured her. "The body's still here." Despite my long history with Peters, I was feeling annoyed at the media invasion of Stratford Court head on the heels of the second body. Still, they had a job to do. Also, I had to stay on reasonably friendly terms with the Fourth Estate because of my day job. "The Chief's inside, too," I added.

But Peters was already setting up her camera on a tripod. "I can talk to him later. It's not often that I actually get to talk to Sebastian McCabe at the scene of the crime."

"Nor will you now," Mac told her. "I must defer to Chief Hummel in this sad matter. However . . ."

He went on for another ten minutes.

Chapter Thirteen
All the Lawyers

Mandy Peters gave about 15 seconds of her two-minute report on the seven o'clock news to "celebrated local mystery writer and amateur sleuth Sebastian McCabe," during which said sleuth expressed his confidence that "the uniqueness of certain circumstances related to these horrific crimes is the very factor that will enable law enforcement to bring the malefactor to justice."

"And what about McCabe's possible role in solving the murders?" asked co-anchor Tammie Tucker at the end of the report. This is the part where the reporter tries to look like the question is coming out of the blue.

"Well, he didn't want to say much about that," Peters reported, pushing hair out of her eyes, "so we'll just have to wait and see."

"Always fascinating to see what Sebastian McCabe will do next," Tucker said with a practiced grin. Considering that Mac once exposed a murderer live during her newscast,[8] I'd say that was an understatement. She moved on to a story about efforts in Cincinnati to remove a statue of the Roman general Cincinnatus because he was probably a slave owner. I surfed over to Channel 11 just in time to catch their

---

[8] See *Bookmarked for Murder* (MX Publishing, 2015).

coverage, which was similar but shorter and the 12-year-old reporter didn't engage in chatter with the anchor.

"They didn't say anything about that language of flowers angle," Lynda kibitzed.

"Mac is trying to lie low, by his standards, and Oscar wouldn't bring it up."

The headline across the top of the *Observer* for Johanna's story the next morning was alliterative and sibilant: **SECOND SISTER SLAIN**. But the article didn't waste any words on poetry. I read it out loud to Lynda, never mind that she'd probably already checked it out online:

> Portia Bainbridge, 42, local civic leader and member of a prominent Erin family, was found slain in her family home Monday afternoon—less than a week after her sister, Ophelia Bainbridge, was bludgeoned to death in the same manner. The sisters were part of a set of triplets. Their father, philanthropist Ezra Bainbridge . . .

"The lead sentence is too long," Lynda opined from the other side of the kitchen, where she was getting milk for cereal out of the refrigerator. But she had to admit that all those facts were important to get upfront. Twelve paragraphs later, before references to Portia's involvement in the Junior League and the Garden Club, Johanna quoted a "friend of the family" as saying that "sibling rivalry was sometimes a contact sport among the Bainbridge girls." Some friend!

Using my phone, I looked up Buck Melonic's story on the CNS website for comparison. It packed a punch: "For the second time in less than a week, the brutal murder of a leading citizen has rocked the small town of Erin, Ohio."

"Poor Ezra," Lynda said in a suitably sepulchral tone of voice. "I can't even imagine the pain of losing one child, let alone two." At that moment our three-year-olds, Sam and Jake, and their five-year-old sister, Donata, were all on reasonably good behavior as they consumed Cheerios.

"Let's hope we never know what it's like," I said.

Donata looked up. "Can we turn on the telly?"

"The telly?" I repeated.

"She's been binge-watching *Peppa Pig*," Lynda said. "Haven't you noticed her British accent?"

After breakfast, as I cleared away the detritus from our meals, Lynda moved on to the horoscopes (Hers: "You will find happiness in helping another;" Mine: "You will not win the lottery today") and then to the crossword puzzle while our offspring discharged energy in the family room.

"What's a five-letter word for 'A place where promises are made'?"

"Altar," I said. And that had me thinking about Devan O'Rourke, Arlo Bainbridge, and Lucius Snedeker the rest of that morning at the office, to no great effect.

After the usual give and take with Popcorn about the Bainbridge case ("Oscar would pull his hair out, if the darling man had any," she assured me), we slogged away for a couple of hours on fine-tuning a new strategic communications plan, writing a Rotary Club speech for GK, and reviewing the draft of a press release by Riley St. Simon, our intern. Mac rescued me from this important but routine work when he called to suggest that we "further explore the Bainbridge family tensions to which Johanna alluded in this morning's story."

"The number of Bainbridges left to be tense is shrinking fast," I quipped.

"Your capacity for dark humor never fails to impress me, Jefferson."

Is that what that was?

"I'd love to know Fleur's unvarnished reaction to Portia's demise," I added.

"She called me this morning to express her shock."

"No doubt." *Call me cynical.*

"Fleur said she regrets that she could never be a real mother to three stepdaughters who were only thirteen years younger than she, and in their thirties, when they first met. Naturally, she hopes that Portia's death will be the end of what she insists are baseless charges that she has neglected and cuckolded her husband."

"Speaking of whom—"

"One would expect that Ezra would be devastated, of course. However, Fleur told me that he appears to be either uncomprehending or in denial, perhaps a mental defense mechanism against the pain."

"Back to Fleur, don't forget that she's not exactly a disinterested observer when it comes to Portia especially."

"Exactly, old boy! That is why I would like to seek the perspective of someone outside the family."

Within the next hour Mac and I were sitting in a matched pair of faux leather visitor chairs in the tastefully appointed office of Phoebe Farleigh, junior partner in Farleigh and Farleigh, the late Portia Bainbridge's counsel in her legal maneuvering against her stepmother.

"You know I can't say very much about my late client," she said.

"Nonsense," Mac cheerfully asserted. "Attorneys frequently say quite a bit about their clients, in public venues as well as in court. It is their clients who are advised to be quiet and let counsel speak for them."

She nodded. "Fair enough, McCabe, but I can't violate attorney-client privilege. Death doesn't end that."

Phoebe Farleigh is a straight shooter—literally as well as figuratively, considering that she's also a member of the WASP gun club. Thirtyish, with soft brown hair and equally brown eyes, her penchant for earth-tone dresses and skirts belies a no-nonsense approach to protecting her client's interests. She was wearing a protective mask with her firm logo, which struck me as being handy for a lawyer who didn't want to give too much away with her facial expressions.

"It cannot have escaped your notice that two combatants in this matter of whether Ezra Bainbridge is being abused by his wife are now dead," Mac said.

"Combatants? I wouldn't use that term. Ophelia Bainbridge may have had an opinion on the matter contrary to her sisters, and she may have been called in by the other parties as a witness, but she was accused of nothing."

"As you would say, fair enough," Mac conceded. For him, that was linguistic slumming. "Still, the two sisters divided by their stepmother have now been united in the manner of their deaths. What do you make of that?"

"I make nothing of it. That's not my job, nor is it yours. I trust the Erin police to sort it all out."

"Unless they arrest somebody who hires you to mount a defense," I parried.

Farleigh had taken the law firm founded by her grandfather into criminal work only a couple of years previously, representing a fellow WASP member in a murder case.[9] She almost smiled at my comment as she looked at her smartwatch. Mac apparently deduced from this subtle clue that she was about to give us the bum's rush. He pushed on:

"I take it, then, that you have no idea who killed your client?"

"None at all."

"Her stepmother should be glad to see her gone, given that they were going at each other in court," I pointed out, somewhat inelegantly but accurately.

After some dead silence to that, Mac asked Farleigh:

"Is it true that Portia Bainbridge obtained through the skullduggery of an employee named Nicole Anderson what she believed to be damnatory evidence against her stepmother in the form of love letters from Fleur Bainbridge's former husband?"

Advice to Oscar Hummel: Do not play poker with Phoebe Farleigh. Not by a twitch of her eyebrows did she betray any surprise that we knew that. And I was looking. Of course, there was that mask.

"You're making an assertion in the form of a question," she said. "Without commenting on the truth or untruth of that assertion, much less your use of the highly loaded and somewhat archaic word 'skullduggery,' why do you even bring that up?"

Sebastian McCabe tried to look wounded. "You misjudge me, Counselor. That really was a question. I will be candid. It was Portia Bainbridge herself who told us that. If she told the truth, without exaggeration, that speaks to how invested she was in pursuing this matter. And perhaps that is not unrelated to her death."

---

[9] See "Foul Ball" in *Murderers' Row* (MX Publishing, 2020).

Farleigh waxed skeptical. "Ophelia and Portia were murdered with the same M.O., presumably by the same killer. What common motive for their deaths could have anything to do with the elder abuse of Ezra Bainbridge, given that the sisters weren't on the same page about that?"

"At this point, the answer to that very good question remains elusive. It occurs to me, however, that the extra-legal length to which Portia Bainbridge went to secure those love letters indicates a personality that would not let anything short of death prevent her from reaching a goal."

The barrister folded her hands on her desk, all business. "Well, that's an interesting psychoanalysis, McCabe, but—to get back to your question—what information my client had and how she came about it is not something I will share at this time. But I can tell you that we do have evidence strongly hinting that Mrs. Bainbridge's devotion to her husband was not total." *Translation: Yeah, we have copies of the love letters, and why would Fleur keep them if she was all-in for Ezra?*

"The elder abuse claims will go forward then, despite Portia's removal from the scene?" Mac asked.

"Frankly, that depends on Arlo Bainbridge. I'm sure that he cares very deeply for his father-in-law, who is also his cousin."

Mac shifted gears. "What can you tell us about David Gunner, your legal adversary in this matter?"

"David? His father's a partner in The Bridges Law Firm, which has represented the Bainbridges forever. They were Bridges & Gunner until shorter names became trendy in the legal profession. Why?"

"He seems to be always on the scene."

"Well, that's partly because he has a lot of business to do with the Bainbridges, but maybe even more because he's besotted with Goldie."

"Whoa!" I said. "Didn't see that one coming."

Farleigh sat back, ready to gossip. "I'm not sure Goldie knows. David's afraid to tell her because he thinks she'll think he's a gold-digger, which is ridiculous. This is all on the QT, understand?"

"Of course," Mac promised. I nodded my agreement.

But I was curious: "If even Goldie doesn't know, how do you know?"

"Late night confidences at Bobbie McGee's Sports Bar. David and I are old friends and law school classmates. He's a good guy and a good lawyer with a bad case this time around. I'm almost sorry I'm going to smack him down, either in court or before it gets that far. Goldie is as enthralled with him as he is with her, by the way, but she's waiting for him to sweep her off her feet. How do I know? WASP talk. Goldie told her mother, her mother told her aunts, and Portia told me."

What a soap opera!

"Speaking of WASP," I said, "don't you find it odd that a tattooed art lover, the doyenne of local society matrons, and an English professor all shot guns together?"

"Not in the least. Everybody needs a hobby."

Farleigh stood up, telegraphing that the interview was over. "I love your books McCabe, and I enjoyed watching you perform magic in that show a few years ago. But I think you've had incredible luck in the amateur sleuthing line up to now. And luck always runs out eventually."

Chapter Fourteen
A Tale Told by an Idiot

Mac's luck held that morning, though. We were still at the offices of Farleigh & Farleigh on Main, just across the street from Daniel's Apothecary, when Oscar summoned us to police headquarters a few blocks away on Court Street. The art deco building, which originally housed the long-gone Fifth National Bank, holds Oscar's small department and a lockup with a few holding cells for the Chief's "guests," as he likes to call them. We arrived to find Oscar in the vault, which he'd turned into an interview room at my suggestion. Sitting across the table from him was a mild-looking man, balding, probably in his early fifties, with thick glasses.

"I suppose you know Danny," Oscar said.

"Of course!" Mac boomed.

Everybody in Erin knows Nathan Daniel, or so I would have thought, although I'm used to seeing him dressed in white rather than the loud Hawaiian shirt he was sporting now. Danny runs the pharmacy half of Daniel's Apothecary while his sister, Jacqui Daniel, is in charge of the 1950s-themed soda fountain and luncheonette.

"He was just telling me that he had a date with Ophelia Bainbridge the day she died," Oscar explained. "He's the man Lucius Snedeker saw."

The Mysterious Stranger! So Snedeker didn't invent the visitor to deflect suspicion from himself.

"I had an appointment for a date, not a date," Daniel corrected. "I went to her house—quite a place, judging by the outside!—and rang the doorbell, but there was no answer. I figured she got cold feet and didn't have the nerve to tell me, so she made herself scarce. Here I was feeling sorry for myself for being ghosted while the poor woman must have already been dead."

"What time was this?" Mac asked.

"Five o'clock on the dot. I'm always prompt."

"Why did it take you almost a week to come forward, Danny?" Oscar asked.

"What he means is," I interpreted, "you were an idiot not to go to the police as soon as you learned she was dead. The big delay makes it look like you had something to hide."

Daniel wiped his forehead with a red paisley handkerchief. "I was discombobulated about the whole deal, for one thing. And for another, I'm kind of embarrassed about using a dating app at my age. But let me tell you, it's not easy for somebody no longer in the first blush of youth to find a person of the opposite sex for companionship."

What I knew about dating apps came second or third hand, but I'd read that Tinder, Bumble, Hinge, and Sparks had enjoyed a big surge in subscriptions because of COVID, in some cases people looking for friendship rather than romance.

Daniel swallowed. "I liked Ophelia a lot. I think maybe it would have worked out."

"Maybe you liked her so much that you got a little too frisky and she didn't like it," Oscar said.

"No!" Daniel's eyes grew huge.

"She pulled away from you, ordered you out of the house, said she never wanted to see you again, and before you knew it, you'd crushed her skull. You didn't mean it; it wasn't premeditated. Manslaughter, not murder."

Oscar sounded like he was just going through the motions, but Nathan Daniel freaked out.

"None of that happened! I wasn't even looking for that. I just wanted somebody that I could talk to who didn't ask about possible drug side effects or, even worse, natter on about some stupid TV show or baseball game."

Oscar, for whom baseball is the eighth sacrament, stared at the pharmacist as if he had been speaking Urdu.

Mac decided to play good cop: "Did you see anyone leaving the scene as you approached?"

"No. I've thought about that, and I'm sure I didn't see anybody come from Stratford Court when I drove into the compound. The killer was gone."

"Or he might have still been there," I put in.

Daniel shuddered.

"Did Ophelia say anything to you that, in retrospect, might have any bearing on her murder?" Mac asked. "Paradoxically, she might have shared something with you that she would not have with someone closer to her."

He gave that a think. "I only went out with her once, for lunch the week before. Very low key. The day she was killed I was going to take her shooting and then out for dinner at Malarkey's Pub."

"Shooting?" Oscar echoed. "As in guns?"

Certainly not basketball.

Daniel nodded. "It was one of the things we had in common. We both liked mysteries, too. That's how dating apps work, isn't it—putting together people with things in common? I'd been filling her prescriptions for years, but I never knew those things about her until I used the app."

"Do you also like flowers?" Mac asked.

"Not especially. Why?"

"Surely you've read in the *Observer* that columbines were near Ophelia's dead hand and that rosemary was left with her sister's body?"

"So?"

After a silence, Oscar jumped back in:

"How well did you know Portia Bainbridge?"

"Not well. Same as I know all the Bainbridges—well enough to discuss their prescriptions, comment on the weather, and avoid talking about religion and politics like any smart small businessperson. They're all customers, the Bainbridges, except the third sister. That one gets her drugs somewhere else, either the CVS or online."

"What about Lucius Snedeker?" I asked. "Is he a customer?"

He shook his head. "No."

That cleared up the small matter of why Goldie's father didn't recognize the pharmacist.

"The morning she died, Ophelia had a call from the same phone number that also called Portia the day *she* died," Oscar said. "That number belongs to a burner phone." Mac raised an eyebrow. This was news to us. Oscar must have gotten into Ophelia's phone. "Is it yours?"

"What?" Daniel exclaimed. "Hell, no! I wouldn't even know how to get a burner phone."

"Why isn't your phone number in Ophelia's cell phone, Danny? I would think you two would be talking and

texting each other if you were starting to go out together."
Oscar Hummel, dating expert.

"We communicated through the dating app, Sparks. What's with all these questions? I'm beginning to think I did the wrong thing by coming forward to help. This is a case of 'no good deed goes unpunished.'"

"You did the right thing," Oscar assured him, "just not at the right time. But better late than never. I don't have any more questions. You're free to go." He didn't add "don't leave town," which would have been a laugh line.

In the rump session after the pharmacist left, Oscar slumped into his office chair. "Well, there go two leads at once—the 'D' for Danny in Ophelia's calendar and the man Snedeker saw 'hanging around' her house."

"You do not put great credence in your theory of a thwarted sexual assault?" Mac asked.

"Not really, no. I can't rule it out, but obviously the only way it works is if Portia's killer was a copycat."

"And a copycat most likely would have copied the columbines at the scene of the first murder, not used rosemary," Mac mused. "A pretty problem, is it not?"

"I don't think 'pretty' is the word Oscar had in mind," I noted to Mac as we left.

"His reaction was most unseemly. I have seldom heard him use such colorful language."

"You can't blame him for being a little frustrated. His hopes that Ophelia's murder was a simple botched burglary have gone belly up, much like Danny's love life."

Before Mac could comment on my artful simile, I said, "Uh-oh."

Across the street and heading our way was our pipe-smoking friend Buck Melonic.

"Morning, gents!" he hailed. "Been talking to the Chief?"

"It would be foolish to deny it," Mac said.

"What did he have for you?"

"You had better ask the Chief."

"Oh, come on, give! We writers and amateur sleuths need to stick together. I promise to spell your name right. Has he found the man seen outside the victim's house on the day of the murder? And what's the meaning of the flower clues? I've decided to call this 'the flower murders' in my stories."

Mac flinched. "Am I right in believing that you were on your way to see Chief Hummel, Mr. Melonic? Very well, then. By all means do so."

He bowed and lumbered off.

"My blushes, Jefferson," he said back in his boat-sized car, "that man chafes me like a shoe that is too tight."

"Unfortunately, he seems to fit Johanna just right," I observed.

Chapter Fifteen
Loved Not Wisely But Too Well

We sat there in Mac's car for a while, thinking out loud. I was also choking on cigar fumes.

"As a general rule, the second murder at the same hands should clarify matters by making the motive obvious," Mac said. "In this case, the opposite seems to be the case."

"Money seems like such a good bet for the motive because the Bainbridges have so much of it," I mused. "Goldie gets her Aunt Ophelia's money—and her cats!—but presumably not Aunt Portia's. And you don't think a copycat killer would depart from the pattern of the first murder by leaving a different flower. So, what do we do now?"

"Visit Arlo Bainbridge."

It only took me a few seconds to come up with an Arlo-as-Killer scenario: "It probably wouldn't be a money motive, although Frank said he 'dabbles' in day trading, which can be as good a way to lose your patchwork shirt as any. But let's say it's love: Arlo has been stepping out on Portia, and Ophelia found out. He killed her to keep her quiet. Hey, wait! Maybe he was stepping out with Ophelia!" *I'm on fire, baby!*

Mac cocked an eyebrow. "That theory would seem to be undercut by her use of the dating app."

"Not at all. Just the opposite! Seeing the evil of her ways, she dumped Arlo and moved on. That made her a threat to him because she could tell her sister at any time."

"And then, after having committed homicide to keep his guilty secret from Portia, Arlo Bainbridge killed Portia?"

"Maybe she figured out that he killed her sister. Or maybe murder is habit-forming if you think you've gotten away with it once."

"And the flowers?"

I waved my hands airily. "A ruse, a red herring, a distraction. Something to throw you off the scent, knowing full well it's just the sort of thing that you would be all-in on because it's like something in one of your mystery novels."

"Ingenious, old boy!" Mac praised.

"I sense a 'however' coming."

"However, it is almost too good to be true."

"I still can't believe it," Arlo said. "This doesn't happen to people like us, to Bainbridges. And I was only gone from the house a short time, maybe an hour. I went to see a man about a 1929 Duesenberg, a beautiful car in cherry shape. I was going to buy it, but now . . ."

His voice trailed off.

We sat in his wood-and-leather den, decorated with models and photos of classic cars.

"Perhaps someone was watching your home to seize the opportunity when you departed," Mac suggested. "Did you notice anyone unknown to you in Stratford Court at the time you left?"

"Notice? No." He shook his head.

"Chief Hummel says that someone called Portia the day she died on what is known as a 'burner' phone, meaning it cannot be traced. Do you have any knowledge of your wife receiving a phone call that day?"

"No. It must have been while I was out." He looked at Mac hard. "Why are you here again, anyway?"

"We thought that perhaps by now you have thought of someone who might have wanted to kill both your sister-in-law and Portia."

"The Chief asked me that yesterday."

"That was yesterday," I snapped. Arlo Bainbridge annoyed me. He gave off vibes that his wife's murder was extremely inconvenient to him, which he took personally.

"Well, the answer is the same today, Cody: I can't think of why anybody would kill either one, much less both. They were pillars of this community, as Bainbridges have been for almost two hundred years."

"You were on good terms with Ophelia?" Mac asked.

"Yeah, we always got along, even when we were kids growing up cousins. Hell, I used to get her to help me with my homework way back in grade school. She was two grades below me, but smarter and willing to work with me."

"There were certain tensions between her and Portia, however."

"That was just sibling stuff. Nothing that a few hours of shooting targets couldn't smooth over. Seemed to work for them. I hate guns myself." *You prefer blunt force trauma?*

"Are you going forward with Portia's claims of elder abuse against her stepmother?" I asked, just to remind everybody I was there.

"No way," Arlo said. "That was her project, which she dragged Des into. It's over, as far as I'm concerned."

"You think your wife's suspicions had no merit, then?" Mac asked.

Arlo Bainbridge's better angels and his demons struggled with each other, judging by the look on his face, and even now I'm not sure which won. But he decided to share a Bainbridge family secret.

"It was never about Ezra," he declared.

The McCabe eyebrows shot up. "No? What, then?"

"Not what—who. It was all about Fleur. Portia thought I didn't know this, but she was in love with Rory Campbell before Fleur snapped him up as her first husband. He was handsome and successful in those days before he went down the bottle. I caught Portia on the rebound—and it was a good catch, let me tell you." He paused for a moment, his eyes glistening. "You would think Rory's well-known unfaithfulness to Fleur and his drinking, both of which had a hand in their divorce, would make Portia feel like she dodged a bullet. I'm not as charming as Rory at his best, but I'm as faithful as a hound dog. I guess that didn't matter to Portia, though. She couldn't get over Rory preferring Fleur to her."

"In that case, her animus toward Fleur was not truly based on unrequited love for Mr. Campbell," Mac stated.

"Who knows? Maybe there was that, too. Who even knows what love is? I sure don't. But I do know this for damned sure: Love isn't everything, especially for marriage. Half the guys in my fraternity who married the girl they were head over heels in love with didn't make it over the finish line. Either the passion burned out, or they found a new passion. I know Portia rubbed some people the wrong way, but she suited me like a 1930 Ruxton Roadster. Why the hell am I telling you this?"

I can think of a reason, Arlo, given that you might be a suspect in Portia's murder. Great simile, by the way.

"Do you have any notion, no matter how unlikely, why flowers were associated with the bodies of both your wife and your sister-in-law?" Mac asked.

"I understand the plant found by Portia was rosemary. I don't know much about gardens and such, but I've heard of rosemary, and I know it's an herb, not a flower."

"Indeed, it is an herb. However, it is also a bush with flowers. Therefore, both Bainbridge women's deaths were associated with flowers. That must have some meaning."

He shook his head in a manner I would call woeful. "If you say so. I have no idea. All I know is I'd never seen that plant before. At least, I don't think so. Like I said, I'm not much on gardening."

"You have a gardener for that," I inserted.

"I wouldn't say that I have a gardener," he hastened to clarify. "Ezra hired and paid Snedeker on all our behalf, mostly to work in the English garden. Probably out of guilt."

"Because Ezra forced Des to have her marriage to him annulled, you mean," Mac speculated.

"So you know about that? I guess everybody does. A small town full of small minds!"

Mac let that pass. Arlo had a right to be a little edgy.

"At any rate, Mr. Bainbridge, Lucius Snedeker is a man with whom, we are given to understand, your wife spent a lot of time."

"She also spent a lot of time with the cook."

"Touché! It does occur to one that if anyone would choose to 'say it with flowers,' in the words of an old advertising slogan, that person would be a gardener."

"Would it?"

"You don't really think Lucius Snedeker looks good for this, do you?" I asked Mac as I buckled my seatbelt back in the car.

"By no means, old boy! I was simply rattling Mr. Bainbridge's cage to see if he would roar."

"He didn't."

"Manifestly not. He betrayed no hint that he suspected anything other than a professional relationship between his wife and Mr. Snedeker. That is important because he was clearly enamored of his wife."

"So he said. In fact, so he went out of his way to say, which seemed suspicious to me. He compared her to a car!"

"High praise from him, as I read the man."

"What about him being on good terms with Ophelia?"

"He would hardly have admitted that so freely if your theory of a romantic alliance between them were true."

I saw a straw and I grasped at it:

"If he was so crazy about his wife, that business about her being in love with Rory Campbell must have really rankled."

"Color me skeptical, Jefferson. Why even mention it if that was his motive? At any rate, Portia Bainbridge's campaign of vengeance against her stepmother appears to have been fed by ego, not romantic jealousy."

"So says Arlo!"

The hirsute McCabe visage looked thoughtful as he gazed at the English garden in the center of Stratford Court. "Mr. Campbell did cause quite a ruckus at the garden party a few weeks ago. And, by thunder, he does work for Bruce Gordon's flower shop! We should speak with him."

But another murder came before we had a chance.

Chapter Sixteen

I Would Give You Some Violets

THIRD TRIPLET SISTER SLAIN

By Johanna Rawls

For the third time in a week, a member of the prominent Bainbridge family was found bludgeoned to death in her own home in the family's Stratford Court compound—the last of the triplet daughters of family patriarch Ezra Bainbridge.

The latest victim was Desdemona Bainbridge, 42, a prominent supporter of the arts and artists in Erin. Her head was crushed in by a bronze figurine and violets were scattered near the body, echoing the two previous murders in which flowers also featured.

Gamaliel Taylor, artist-in-residence at the Shinkle Museum of Art, of which Ms. Bainbridge was a major patron, told police he became concerned when he arrived at the home for an appointment at 8 p.m. Tuesday and there was no answer at the door. He called 911.

"My officers are working overtime on this case with the assistance of the Ohio Bureau of Criminal Investigation," said Erin Police Chief Oscar Hummel. "We intend to reach out for all the help we need."

That was the beginning of the story stretched across the top of the *Observer & News-Ledger* on Wednesday morning. By that time Oscar had already "reached out" (a cliché I hate) to Sebastian McCabe the night before.

"Hell's bells!" Oscar exploded as we arrived at Des's painted lady residence. "This is your kind of case, only you're not coming through." We were among the first to get there, ahead of the coroner. The body lay in the living room, sprawled in an unnatural position in front of the fireplace, with a bloody head and violets decorating the corpse.

"You have my deepest apologies," Mac told Oscar, in a tone with enough acid to burn through metal. "I am sure the Bainbridge sisters share your disapprobation of me."

"They should," Gamaliel Taylor snarled. He was dressed in shorts and flip-flops, looking more than ever like a beach bum. I don't get that whole three-day-beard-is-sexy thing. "Whatever's going on in this burg is obviously beyond the local cops and their much-vaunted amateur sleuth. It's a disgrace, an outrage. Ezra Bainbridge should hire his own detective force if that's what it takes. He can afford it."

You're either (a) a mass murderer acting pissed to cover your tracks, (b) genuinely upset about what happened to Des because you cared for her, or (c) upset about being thrown off the gravy train while it was still moving.

"I don't need any more from you right now," Oscar informed Taylor. "You can leave. But don't leave town."

Taylor left, tossing angry epithets behind him like hand grenades on his way out.

"The person who finds the body is usually a good suspect," I observed, not for the first time.

Oscar snorted. He looked like he needed a cigarette, which he'd sworn off, or a vape, which Popcorn discouraged. "That doesn't exactly help with three bodies and three different body-finders. Taylor sounded unraveled on the 911 tape—like he was really shocked—but who knows? Maybe he's just a good actor. Maybe they're all good actors. Arlo Bainbridge seemed torn up when he called in his wife's murder."

"Well, Mr. Taylor is an artist, albeit of dubious merit," Mac muttered. "Perhaps he is indeed an actor as well. Art in the blood is liable to take the strangest forms, you know."

His mention of blood drew my eyes back to the body. There was plenty of blood there. "The murderer really hated all three sisters enough to go beyond the call of duty in smashing their heads, or wants us to think so, or is just a vicious bastard," I said. "Take your pick."

But Mac didn't pick. With his hands in nitrile gloves provided by Gibbons, he was examining the murder weapon, an art deco-ish bronze statue of a dancer. "This is signed by the artist Erté, whose real name was Romain de Tirtoff. Kate is fond of his work. It must be relatively valuable, just like the other two murder weapons. Curious, that." We learned later the Erté was worth about $6,200—not pocket change unless your name is Bainbridge or Gamble.

"And then there are these flowers. Do you notice anything strange about them?"

Oscar and I said "no" at almost the same time.

"They're in pretty sad shape, though," I added. "Snedeker must be falling down on the job."

"Exactly, old boy! I might also note that we now have columbine, rosemary, and violets."

And I might have noted that if we had parsley, sage, rosemary, and thyme instead I would suspect Simon and Garfunkel, but I had no chance.

"What's going on here?"

We whirled around to see Goldie Bainbridge tearing through the door of her mother's house, David Gunning trailing behind her.

"I'm sorry," Oscar told her. He didn't need to say anything else.

At first, she just stared. Then her eyes filled with water. She buried her head in her hands and let go. The sound of her sobs wrenched my heart. Gunning hesitated, then put his arms around her, and she collapsed into him.

When she could finally talk, she said: "This is going to kill Grandpa." She lapsed into crying again.

"I don't want to bother you with a lot of questions at this time," Oscar said after he let that play out a while. "I take it that you've been living with your mother lately but were gone this evening."

Goldie nodded. "We had a long workday, so David and I and a few others from the office stopped by Gatsby's to unwind a little." This was a new drinkery in the location formerly occupied by The Speakeasy, which had gone out of business after COVID and a murder.[10]

---

[10] See *No Ghosts Need Apply* (MX Publishing, 2021).

"Do you notice anything in this room, anything missing, anything added?"

She looked around, taking her time, then shook her head. "No. Nothing. Wait! Those violets. I don't know where they came from."

"Okay," Oscar said. "Your mother had an appointment with Gamaliel Taylor at eight o'clock, according to him. There were no signs of a break-in when my officers found the body. In fact, the door was unlocked. Was your mother meeting anyone else here this afternoon?"

"Not that I know of, but then I wouldn't necessarily know. I didn't know Gamaliel was coming over, for instance. But he's here a lot on Shinkle business."

Not monkey business? This seemed an indelicate time to ask, what with Des's dead body still in the room.

"Was your mother romantically involved with Mr. Taylor?" Mac asked. So much for delicacy.

Oscar gave him the stink eye for interrupting.

"What!" Goldie said. "Don't be icky. He's closer to Grandpa's age than to Mom's."

"The reason I asked about your mother meeting anyone that afternoon," Oscar said, reasserting himself, "is that whoever killed her must have been somebody she opened the door for—somebody who was beyond suspicion even though her sisters had been murdered in their homes."

"No one is beyond suspicion in this sad affair," Mac said. He turned to Goldie. "I am rather surprised that your grandfather or your mother did not hire guards for Stratford Court after the second murder. That is certainly not beyond the family's financial resources."

"I advised them to," Gunner spoke up. "Des said that smacked of white privilege and that she wasn't afraid. Ezra said he wouldn't turn Stratford Court into an armed compound, but Fleur was arranging to do it anyway. She just didn't move fast enough."

This was news to Goldie, judging by the expression on her beautiful, tear-stained face. Gunner was the family attorney who probably knew a lot of things that didn't filter down to the younger Bainbridges. But why didn't he mention that particular factoid to the woman he was sweet on and who worked in his office? It wasn't legal business and therefore work-related, so maybe he thought it would be inappropriate to spill the beans that Mrs. Bainbridge was acting against her husband's wishes.

"My people and the coroner's office are going to be busy here for a while tonight," Oscar told Goldie. "It might be best if you take some clothes and leave. Do you have a place to stay? Maybe somebody to stay with you?"

Gunner looked like he wanted to volunteer. It occurred to me that whatever benefitted Goldie financially could wind up in a joint checking account if those two commingled their lives and their finances. I made a mental note of that.

She nodded. "I have my own apartment on College Street. Most of my clothes are there. I'll be fine, or as good as I can be."

Oscar asked her to stop by the police station at her convenience on Wednesday for a routine interview. She agreed and left, Gunner in tow.

"Hard to believe she had anything to do with her mother's death," Oscar said in their wake.

"Don't be a sentimentalist," I chided him. "She's more-than-pretty but her name is Marigold, which is a flower, and she inherits from both her aunt and her mother." Never mind that Popcorn called her "a sweet kid."

"She was with Gunner all afternoon."

I snorted. "That's no alibi, Oscar. If she told him to jump, he'd ask how high on his way up."

"You posit then that the murder of Portia Bainbridge was merely a red herring?" Mac said.

Inspiration struck. "Maybe Goldie and Arlo are in it together! She killed his and he killed hers—the old *Strangers on a Train* scenario. Gunner didn't even have to be in on it."

That sounded pretty good to me, especially since I was just spitballing it. I didn't even know what I was going to come out of my mouth until it did.

"Really, Jefferson, I must say—"

But he didn't say. He stopped dead, silenced by the sound of shouting coming from outside.

"Now what?" Oscar grumbled.

He yanked open the front door. Lucius Snedeker and Officer Mentzel were dialoging loudly in each other's faces, social distancing clearly not on their minds. We stepped out a few feet on the front walk to watch and listen.

"I want to see her!" the gardener yelled, looking nothing like the chilled weekend-rocker of a few days before. His eyes were wild, and he was clenching his fists. "She's the mother of my child."

"I'm sorry for your loss, sir," Mentzel said, politely but at a high decibel level. "But I'm only going to tell you one more time: This is a crime scene, and you have to leave."

He started to argue back until Oscar called his name. "Mr. Snedeker!"

He whirled in our direction. "Chief, you've got to let me see her."

"What I've got to do is protect the crime scene," Oscar fired back. "I gave Officer Mentzel orders to admit your daughter as an exception because she's been living here and I wanted to see if she noticed anything different. How did you know what happened?"

"Goldie texted me."

"Perhaps you should be with her," Mac said. "She could use a father right now."

"Who the hell are you to say?"

"Point taken," said with a slight bow, was a major concession for Sebastian McCabe, although I doubt that Snedeker appreciated it.

"Enough talk," Oscar announced. "You're going to leave on your own power or be escorted out."

Snedeker rushed toward the door. Oscar, moving fast for a guy his size, blocked him. "I'm going to cut you a little slack in the circumstances and not arrest you for interfering in a criminal investigation. Providing you *leave now.*" His voice rose on the last two words.

Angry beyond words, Snedeker huffed off without saying anything else.

"Have you examined Desdemona's cell phone?" Mac asked Oscar in his wake.

The Chief looked like he'd rather not think too hard about that memory. "Yeah. Facial recognition. Gibbons helped me. Don't tell the coroner I moved the body slightly. Anyway, she did have a call from a burner phone, if that's what you're thinking. Two, in fact. One yesterday."

Before Mac could comment on that, Arly Eppensteiner entered the crime scene without knocking. I found out later the coroner had been pulled from a dinner for donors to her children's school, at which she'd been giving a speech.

"I'm your relief," she told Mac. "You can leave now."

Mac glanced at Oscar, who shrugged as if to say, "Out of my hands." So he bowed to the coroner, deeper than he had to Snedeker. "I do not believe I have ever been thrown out of a place with greater grace, Dr. Eppensteiner."

"You're welcome." She looked at the body and shook her head full of dark curls. "I never get used to this."

We walked in the English garden for a while, Mac chewing on an unlit cigar. It was a hot and humid night, typical for August in southern Ohio even though September was almost upon us.

"You should talk to your 'client,' Ezra," I said.

"I have not the heart to do so yet, old boy."

There was nothing I could say to that.

"Maybe it was Gunner, not Goldie," I suggested after a while. "Maybe she's as sweet as she seems and totally innocent in these murders. If the family legal eagle walks her down the aisle—a quaint activity these days, I grant you—her status as a double heiress will benefit him."

He stopped and regarded me. "She would have to be involved under that scenario."

"Why?"

"Because she is his alibi for her mother's murder."

"Oh. Right."

"Do you know what this garden is missing, old boy?"

I looked around. "There's something missing? There must be dozens of different kinds of flower here."

"Quite so, but none of *genus* viola. That is to say, violets. Unlike the Sherlock Holmes canon, which is full of women named Violet, there are no violets in this garden.

Therefore, the violets spread on Desdemona Bainbridge's corpse came from somewhere else. You realize what that means, of course?"

"Um, sure I do. But tell me anyway just so you can feel useful."

"If the killer did not merely grab a flower that was at hand, that means *the particular kind of flower must have some significance, not just the idea of a flower in general.*"

"Hmph! Violets are practically a weed around here, if that means anything. Lynda keeps digging them out of our backyard."

"But those unwelcome volunteers are not African violets, which are the species we just saw on Desdemona's body," Mac informed me. "In this part of the country, one would have to go to a greenhouse to obtain African violets."

How does he know this stuff? By reading almost everything and forgetting almost nothing. And yet, in the end it turned out that even the massive McCabe mind overlooked something for far too long in this case.

"African violets," I repeated. "That's good, right? Gibbons can put out an alert, or whatever it's called, and have his counterparts within a fifty-mile radius or so in Ohio and Kentucky looking for a greenhouse purchase by somebody close to the Bainbridge sisters."

"As indicated by the name on the credit card?" He nodded. "Yes, that is certainly worth the attempt, presuming that the killer would be so foolish as to not pay by cash."

"Cash? Is that even a thing anymore?"

Mac ignored my question. "There is, of course, an individual who works for a florist and whose relationship with the Bainbridges is fraught to say the least."

Chapter Seventeen
The Sticking Place

The next morning, the day Erin awoke to the "Third Triplet Sister Slain" headline, we went to see Rory Campbell at the Mulberry Street flower shop of long-time city council member Bruce Gordon. The Gordon greenhouses are in a separate location, a few miles from downtown. Campbell was behind the counter and the prickly Gordon, whom I've always suspected likes plants much more than he likes people, was nowhere in evidence.

Campbell looked up from checking his phone and saw us approaching. "What took you so long?" he asked. "I know you're not here to buy pansies." He was sober, unlike the day of the garden party at Stratford Court, and his hair wasn't such a mess, but I would have recognized him. He was about Mac's height, five-ten, with wire-rimmed glasses. His face might have been handsome once; now it was just sad.

Mac raised an eyebrow.

Campbell signaled to another employee and silently asked her to take his place while he walked with us. He took us out back, where plants and planters were for sale during warm months in a kind of brick courtyard.

"Officer Lehmann from the Erin police already paid me a visit the day after Portia was killed," Campbell said. "I figured you'd be right behind. Undoubtedly you heard that the last time I saw Portia alive we had a blow-up, and I made a complete fool out of myself in front of an audience that included Lehmann."

"And us," I said helpfully. "We were there, too."

Campbell closed his eyes. I could almost hear him pray *Give me strength.*

"It borders on a cliché, does it not?" Mac said. "The murder victim in a public argument before her death. And yet, Portia Bainbridge's murder was three weeks after that regrettable incident. It is hardly credible that you waited that long to slay her in a paroxysm of enraged passion."

"Enraged? Hell, I didn't even blame her for being pissed, once I sobered up," Campbell averred. "I brought flowers to the party, but I was really a gatecrasher."

"Why did you do it?" I asked.

"I was in the midst of a drinking relapse at the time, and not exactly thinking clearly. I guess I just wanted to see Fleur again. I was married to Fleur, you know. I left her for another woman—biggest mistake of my life, and I'd say that even if my second wife didn't leave *me* for another woman. Fleur is a wonderful person."

"Before your marriage to her you were romantically involved with Portia," Mac reminded him.

"How the hell did you know that? Yeah, we had a good thing, but it was a short thing. Portia didn't wear well with me. Too controlling, and too hoity-toity. And she didn't take it well when I moved on."

"Moved on to Fleur, in fact. It has been suggested that is why Portia accused her stepmother of elder abuse—a long-held grudge against her for winning your affections."

"I wouldn't put it past her, frankly. Not to speak ill of the dead." *But you are speaking ill of the dead, Rory.*

"Are you aware that Mrs. Bainbridge kept your love letters?"

He shrugged. "As I said, she didn't take it well when I decided I had enough of her."

"Excuse the confusion," Mac said. "I referred to Mrs. Fleur Bainbridge, not Mrs. Portia Bainbridge."

The ghost of a smile played at the corners of Campbell's mouth. "Really? She saved my letters?"

"You did not know that?"

"I had no idea. Fleur hasn't been any more than coolly polite to me since the divorce. I can't blame her. It's not like the Bainbridges socialize with a guy who works at the floral shop."

"And why do you?" I spared Mac from asking. "You're an ear, nose, and throat specialist."

"Was," he corrected. "I got too handy with my hands when I was in my cups. I wasn't on duty at the time, but St. Hildegarde Health quite rightly suggested that I resign." He sighed. "It was just as well. The pressure to see more patients and fill out more records on the computer had a lot to do with my bottle problem. That's oversimplifying a bit, but not entirely. Anyway"—he looked around at the plants—"I'm not all that sorry to get out of the medical rat race, and I've always loved flowers. I became a doctor to help people. I like to think that I still help people."

"And yet, by your own account, you remain prey to over-imbibing," Mac said.

"I told you that was a relapse, brought on by I-don't-know-what—hearing about the garden party, maybe. Anyway, I'm in AA. In fact, I was either at a lunch-time AA meeting or here at work when Portia was killed," depending on when it happened."

"In other words, you have a convenient alibi."

Campbell's face reddened and his voice rose. "Convenient or not, I can prove I wasn't at Stratford Court that day. I already told Lehmann that."

Another solid alibi! Can I help it if the Cody brain cycled back to *Strangers on a Train* and the old "I'll kill yours if you kill mine" scenario?

When neither Mac nor I reacted to this outburst, the doctor-florist calmed down enough to say in a deliberately composed voice: "I'd better get back to work. Unless maybe you'd like to buy something."

This last was a taunt, so maybe he was surprised when Mac replied:

"As it happens, I would like to purchase an African violet."

Campbell shook his head. "We don't have any."

"Did you just sell out?"

"No, we don't keep them in stock. They aren't very popular around here."

They were with somebody.

"Why African violets on the corpse when the kind we have around here are so common it's hard not to find them in your yard?" I asked Mac out on the sidewalk.

"Perhaps the killer was not from 'around here'," Mac suggested.

"Taylor, you mean? What possible reason would he have for murdering Des, much less her sisters?"

"How the devil can I know, Jefferson! This infernal case is a farrago of possibilities and hardly any certainties." Heads turned our way at the raised voice. Mac shut up. After a few moments of thoughtful silence, he resumed in a lower voice as we walked to the car. "It is time for a mental reset. In our previous investigations I have often asked what changed as a result of the murder. Perhaps in this matter, we should pay attention to what changed *before* the murder. For one thing, Gamaliel Taylor entered the scene."

"You're about to say that he's worth a visit, which may be true. But I need to put in a guest appearance at my office. Even Popcorn needs supervision now and then. We're trying to ride herd on a *Wall Street Journal* reporter doing a story about robots on campus."

"Some new initiative in the School of Engineering?"

"No, one of the food-delivery services is using this cute six-wheeled rover made in Russia to get chow to dorms across the country. SBU is one of about 250 colleges and universities in the test market."

"Let us pray there are no mishaps. That would not be what I believe is called 'good press.'"

The "made in Russia" angle became a problem after the invasion of Ukraine, but that was six months in the future.

When I got to my HQ on the fourth floor of the Gamble Building, Popcorn was in full panic mode, and not about robots on campus.

"Thank God you're here Jeff," she said. "Oscar needs you—and fast."

I was pretty sure he didn't want me to join his Wednesday night poker game.

"Did he call me?" I thought maybe my cell phone was on the fritz.

"He will. He asked me for what I would call PR advice, and I told him he needed to move up the food chain."

"That's nice, but why in the world does Oscar—"

My phone rang. It was Oscar.

"What's the problem?" I said, by way of greeting.

"I'm supposed to go into a news conference with Sutterlee and Slade in fifteen minutes."

The Reverend Fred Sutterlee, senior pastor of Erin's Apostolic Holiness Church of the Holy Spirit and Erin's first black mayor, was running for a second term in the November election. Marvin Slade, you may recall, is our elected county prosecutor.

"Why is that a problem?" I asked. Oscar is no stranger to dueling with media, whether they are prowling alone or in packs.

"Politics," he said bitterly. "Slade is really pressuring me to solve the Bainbridge murders, and I mean yesterday. Not coincidentally, Ezra Bainbridge is one of his big financial backers."

"Oh."

Slade was just re-elected for the umpteenth time in the 2020 election, and the persistent rumors that he was gunning for higher office were stronger than ever. He would need a big war chest to run for Congress or state office.

"What am I supposed to say that isn't a lie and makes the prosecutor look good, Jeff?"

"He isn't your boss," I reminded Oscar, who reports to the mayor and city council. "I'm not sure that making him look good is in your job description."

"But I have to work with him."

"Okay, then, here's the Cody advice: It wouldn't hurt to start with an expression of sympathy for the Bainbridge family. After that, tread carefully. Don't say anything that might come back to haunt you, because video lasts forever, just like the ten-year-old tweets that forced Bill Tanner to drop out of the city council race two years ago. By that I mean, take your time in answering questions and make sure you get all your facts straight so that nobody focuses in on some minor misstatement and misses your bigger point. That happens to politicos all the time. And speaking of politicos, don't make any promises you can't keep. Understate rather than overstate; it will make you look better later." *Hey, that's not bad!* The more I talked, the better I sounded to myself.

"Also, don't let the media pressure you into saying anything you don't want the killer to hear. In other words, don't tip your hand just to show you're on the ball. And don't lose your temper and call a reporter an asshole, despite the temptation."

"I wouldn't call Rawls an asshole." Oscar sounded wounded.

"That's because she isn't one, even if she has to ask you some tough questions. But I assume she isn't why you called me. At a news conference for a high-profile case like this, there could be media from all over the country."

"Oh, joy."

I looked over at Popcorn. "Did I miss anything?"

She grabbed my phone. "Wear your official hat, honey, not the Erin Eagles cap." Then she and my phone walked out of my office, apparently so that she could whisper sweet nothings to "honey" in privacy. I decided right then not to comment on that afterwards, in the interest of office harmony.

The news conference was livestreamed by TV4 Action News. I alerted Mac and we each watched it on our separate computers from the comfort of our respective offices. I could occasionally hear Popcorn in the outer office vigorously expressing her opinion as the drama unfolded. She is an extrovert who tends to process out loud.

Oscar, standing between Reverend Mayor Sutterlee and Marvin Slade in some big room at the county building (Slade's turf), looked like a prisoner of war.

The mayor began by welcoming everyone, then dove in. "The purpose of this joint news conference," he said, "is to assure the citizens of our community that the full energies of our fine police department and the county prosecutor are devoted to bringing to justice the killer that is stalking one of our finest families."

Reverend Sutterlee is a rotund man whose political speeches sound like sermons, and whose sermons sound like political speeches. He's a force of nature, full of energy and optimism, who spends some of his spare time singing with a priest and a rabbi in a trio of tenors known as Joyful Noise. With the stage setting out of the way, he turned the microphone over to Oscar.

"I want to, first of all, express my sympathy to the remaining members of the Bainbridge family," he said. "These heinous crimes have touched all of Erin, but, obviously, them most of all. And it is with them in mind that our officers have been putting in extra hours every day to track down every lead."

Not too bad. I held my breath here, though, hoping he wouldn't point out that with every murder there were more clues. Although that was true, calling attention to the mounting number of homicides wouldn't be a good move. But Oscar dodged that particular bullet, moving on to say that his officers had conducted two dozen interviews.

"Do you think the killer may be among the persons you've interviewed?" asked TV4's own Mandy Peters.

"We think the killer may be anyone."

"Will you be increasing patrols at Stratford Court?" Johanna wanted to know.

"We've already done that, effective this morning."

Locking the barn door after the third cow has been slain.

"Do you see any significance in the murder weapons all being relatively expensive pieces of artwork?" Buck Melonic asked Oscar from his seat right to Johanna.

"I'd rather not comment on that." Probably because he never noticed it. Maybe Mac should have pointed it out to him. Or maybe it was meaningless.

"Is it true that you have a person of interest who was seen at the home of Ophelia Bainbridge on the day she was killed?" asked Morris Kindle of the Associated Press. *Old news, Morrie!*

"We have interviewed such a person and we do not believe that individual is involved in any of the murders. We no longer consider him a person of interest."

"You said, 'any of the murders,'" Johanna pointed out. "Is there a possibility that more than one killer is involved?"

I was almost sure I could see sweat on Oscar's broad forehead. "We can't rule that out."

"But the triplets were all killed with similar weapons and the killer left flowers in each case," Melonic objected.

Oscar nodded. "I said we couldn't rule out multiple killers. Most likely, there was only one. But a copycat is not beyond the bounds of possibility."

Melonic stuck to the singular with his follow-up question, however: "What message do you think the killer was trying to send?"

"We're not ready to talk about that at this time."

"Why not?"

Ignoring the question, because he had no good answer, Oscar called on the intern from campus radio station WIJC-FM. He was a skinny guy with dark, curly hair who looked like he should wear glasses but didn't.

"Is it true that you've asked SBU's Professor Sebastian McCabe to get involved in the case?" he asked.

Marvin Slade stepped up to the plate for that one, not giving Oscar a chance to obfuscate. Slade has the horn-rimmed glasses the reporter lacked, with dyed brown hair that he carefully combs to hide the bald patches.

"I'm sure the Erin Police Department, with assistance from the Sussex County Sheriff's Office and the Ohio Bureau of Criminal Investigation, is more than capable of handling these murders without the help of amateurs."

He looked at Oscar as if daring him to disagree. My advice to Oscar was not unheeded, for he thought before he spoke up, and it showed.

"Let there be no doubt," he said after a few moments. "We will identify and arrest the killer, or killers, of Ophelia, Portia, and Desdemona Bainbridge. And Mr. Slade will bring him, or her, or them to justice in a court of law."

With the help of Sebastian McCabe, I thought.

Chapter Eighteen
To Thine Own Self Be True

"Oscar did quite well," Mac judged in our rump session afterwards on the phone.

"It's almost as if he were coached," I quipped.

"Indeed. That question from Mr. Melonic about the murder weapons directs one's attention to the fact that they were all artworks of a sort, as you will recall I previously noted. And Gamaliel Taylor is an artist, of a sort."

"What motive could he possibly have?"

"The question of motives again! Mr. Taylor is an outsider to Erin, potentially a snake in the garden. He might have a motivation that we could not imagine. As a thought experiment, perhaps the Bainbridge sisters shared knowledge of a guilty secret about Mr. Taylor. Or perhaps this is not about the past but about the future—some ambition they could prevent him from achieving."

I waxed skeptical. "All three of them?"

"That is not beyond imagining. Suppose, for example, that he eliminated a threat from Ophelia and Portia, confident that Desdemona would protect him or not believe him to be guilty, and then found that confidence to be misplaced."

"You wouldn't use that in one of your Damon Devlin mysteries, would you?"

He hesitated.

"I didn't think so," I said. "Let's see what O'Neill knows about Taylor. But first I have to deal with that pesky *WSJ* reporter."

After I provided some relevant facts and figures about food-delivering rovers on campus to a friendly journalist (i.e., one who was not writing a story that would offend anyone who wrote checks to the university), Mac and I called on Dr. Dante Peter O'Neill.

"I'm reliably informed that Gamaliel Taylor is a big fan of Gamaliel Taylor," reported the Dean of SBU's School of Arts and Humanities. "That puts him in select company. He is far from being a well-known or well-regarded artist."

Tell me something I don't know, Dante. O'Neill's own background is in the fine arts as a painter, but apparently not the avant-garde kind because he likes three-piece suits. At six-five, he tops me by four inches. He wears roundish glasses and sports a thin mustache barely visible against his dark skin.

"In fact," O'Neill continued, "when he was announced as the Shinkle's first artist-in-residence, I'd never heard of him before. And since I had recommended to the committee a few other names for the post that I thought would be excellent, I was naturally curious about the successful applicant. So, I made inquiries. It seems that he is best known in the arts community—to the limited extent that he is known at all—as a womanizer."

Mac raised an eyebrow. "Surely that term is almost archaic in this licentious age."

"So is Taylor. Archaic, I mean. He's in his mid-sixties, but he specializes in painting well-endowed female nudes using what gossip says are what you might call 'models with benefits.' I wouldn't trust the man near my daughter."

"How old is she?" I asked, irrelevantly.

O'Neill sighed. "Eighteen."

"Why did the artist-in-residence committee choose the libidinous Mr. Taylor?" Mac asked.

"I don't know. It didn't seem right for me to ask, given that I had my own candidates."

"Who headed the committee?"

"The same person who came up with the idea, provided the initial funding, and led the fundraising effort to keep the program going—Des Bainbridge. I heard scuttlebutt from a committee member that Adam Mendenhall resisted the appointment in his capacity as museum director, but eventually had to cave in."

Gamaliel Taylor lived in an Airstream travel camper parked at a camp along the river about five miles outside of Erin city limits. It was silver and rounded on the outside, and spacious enough on the inside to sleep five. If he bought it new, he paid north of $165,000. I looked that up.

"I enjoy the freedom of movement this choice of abode gives me," he said, not that we asked. "As soon as I fulfill my commitment to the Shinkle I'll be on my way east, and not a moment too soon."

We were sitting at a built-in table in the kitchenette area. It was spacious enough even for the considerable girth of Sebastian McCabe. As for Taylor, his clothes hung loosely on him, and I again had the feeling that he had lost weight.

"How did you meet Desdemona Bainbridge?" Mac asked.

Taylor looked like he smelled something bad, and we were it. "Why should I answer such a personal question from you, McCabe?"

"Why should you not? Presumably, we share the desire to solve the murder of the Bainbridge sisters."

In a gesture that reminded me of Goldie, Taylor put his head in his hands. No sobs came out, but when he looked up again his eyes were moist. If he was acting, he was good at it. But he could have been good at it.

"Des and I first met earlier this year during an online conference of the national non-profit Arts Connections," he said in a listless tone. "That was where I heard about the Shinkle's artist-in-residence opening. Des was surprised to learn that I'd even heard of Erin, and much more so that I'd been here many years ago. I encouraged her to become familiar with my work. In all modesty, I must say that she became quite enamored of my neo-realistic style. We quickly developed a rapport. I came to Erin several times to meet with her and share my ideas about encouraging the arts."

"Is that all you shared?" I asked. Somebody had to, although I tried not to leer.

"I find your insinuation insulting." Taylor appeared to be seconds away from slapping me with a white glove and demanding a duel. Maybe it was the ponytail.

"You have a certain reputation along that line, Mr. Taylor," Mac pointed out.

"And you have a reputation as an amateur detective, but I'm not seeing any evidence of it."

If words could cut, there would be blood on the floor right now.

"You deflect the question. Was your relationship with Desdemona Bainbridge personal?"

Taylor stopped fencing. "Personal, yes; I might even say highly personal. But not sexual. That would be a bridge too far, not that it's any of your business. I'm devastated by the loss of all the Bainbridge sisters."

"You knew them all?"

"More or less."

"They didn't always get along," I said, just to see if he seized the chance to dis Ophelia. He didn't.

"Families are complicated," Taylor said with a shrug.

"Do you have any idea who killed the Bainbridges?" Mac asked.

"If you're expecting me to take a swipe at Fleur, forget it." He spoke with some heat.

"I have no expectations."

"I've never spoken with the woman, but even if Des was right about her, why would Fleur kill Ophelia? Whoever did the murders must have had it in for all three of them. I have no idea who that could be. If I did, I'd kill him with my bare hands."

"There has been quite enough killing," Mac said.

"Words are cheap even with inflation run rampant," I told Mac when we were out of Taylor's listening range, "but he did seem thrown for a loop by the murders."

But Mac's thoughts were on flowers. "Columbine, rosemary, and violets. How are they linked? What message is the killer trying to send?"

"I don't know, but I hope the message is finished."

"What do you mean, Jefferson?"

"We're out of triplets, but not out of Bainbridges."

Chapter Nineteen
Nothing Will Come of Nothing

Cincinnati's TV4 Action News led the newscast that night with Oscar's news conference. After a few selected soundbites, including one of Slade assuring reporters that the Chief was "more than capable of handling these murders without the help of amateurs," Mandy Peters ended her report by saying: "And tonight, Brian, Chief Hummel tells me there is still no person of interest."

Brian Rose, Tammie Tucker's veteran co-anchor, looked serious. That's his job, except when jovial bantering is called for.

"But the investigation is ongoing?" he said.

"Yes, Brian. The Chief tells me that his officers are again going over all evidence from the three murders to try to find connections other than those mysterious flowers left at each murder scene."

"Mysterious indeed," Brian said. He changed the timbre of his voice to signal his switch to a new topic: "The latest numbers show that the COVID-19 vaccination rate continues . . ."

Both the lead paragraph and the headline on Tall Rawls's account in the *Observer* the next day, Thursday, focused on Oscar's promise at the end of the news confab.

CHIEF: WE WILL CATCH KILLER, the headline said. It was fair and accurate and thorough—so much so that a careful reader with a good B.S. detector would realize that there was a lot of hot air blowing at that news conference.

Melonic's story for the Central News Service led with Oscar's non-answer to one of the reporter's news conference questions: "Erin, Ohio Police Chief Oscar Hummel declined Wednesday to speculate on the meaning of flowers left at the bodies of three triplet sisters from a prominent local family murdered in a space of just eight days."

"The media types aren't making Oscar look any too good," Popcorn complained.

That's not their job.

"Oh, I don't know," I said.

"You guys have to solve these murders pronto!"

Now, why didn't we think of that?

"You guys" referred to the fact that Mac, being a tenured professor and having practically nothing to do, had dropped by my office that morning.

"I assure you, that is our fondest wish," Mac assured Popcorn.

"What you need is a big board where you can post photos of the victim and all the suspects," she said. "That's what they do on all those TV shows, like *Vera*—"

"*Death in Paradise*," I threw in.

"*Brokenwood Mysteries*," Popcorn tossed back.

"I do not find that technique particularly promising," Mac said before I could even think of mentioning *Midsomer Murders*. "However, perhaps a relationship chart would reveal something."

"What do you mean?" Popcorn said.

"A matrix showing how the three sisters relate to the other *dramatis personae* in this case. A simple table in a Word document would do if you would be so kind."

We were standing in the outer office, by Popcorn's computer, so she went to work. Within a few minutes, she had the requested table constructed. As dictated by Mac, it looked like this:

THE BAINBRIDGE CONNECTIONS

Relationship	**Ophelia**	**Portia**	**Desdemona**
Ezra	Daughter	Daughter	Daughter
Fleur ("flower")	Defender	Accuser (primary)	Accuser (secondary)
Arlo	Sister-in-law (cousin)	Wife (cousin)	Sister-in-law (cousin)
G. Taylor	?????????????	?????????????	Patron (+?)
L. Snedeker (gardener)	Ex-in-law	Ex-in-law (garden mate)	Ex-wife (friendly)
Marigold (a flower)	Favorite aunt	Aunt	Mother
D. Gunner	Lawyer	Complicated	Complicated (enamored of her daughter)
N. Daniel	Pharmacist/ Date	Pharmacist	?????????????

"I know Gunner is complicated because he's the family lawyer, and in a sense represents all of them, and yet he's on the other side of Portia and Des in the abuse allegations," I said. "But what's with the question marks?"

"Ophelia and Portia knew Gamaliel Taylor, but we do not know how well," Mac expounded. "There is no reason to think they were more than nodding acquaintances. However, we cannot be sure."

"And Danny?"

"Mr. Daniel said that all the Bainbridges were customers of his pharmacy except for Desdemona. However, we do not know whether she knew him in some other context."

"What this doesn't show is the relationships of the sisters to each other," Popcorn pointed out.

"Indeed," Mac said. "By all accounts they had their disagreements, and yet pursued their mutual hobby of target shooting without casualties. I see nothing there."

"I see nothing anywhere," I said. "This chart is a mess." I ticked it off. "Ezra had no reason to kill his daughters. Of course, he could be a lunatic, but he's also confined to a wheelchair most of the time. Fleur had a beef with two of her three stepdaughters, but not the first one killed—in fact, just the opposite. If that's on the table, then so is every other scenario where one or two murders are tossed in just to throw law enforcement off the track. This doesn't clarify anything!"

"What about that sleazy Gamaliel Taylor?" Popcorn asked.

"You have met him?" Mac asked.

"I was relying on Jeff's description."

Taylor had possibilities. "Let's not forget that as a newcomer to Erin, he might not realize that he could dig common violets off of somebody's lawn instead of buying the African variety somewhere," I reminded Mac.

"Maybe he hit Des on the head in a fit of passion," Popcorn offered. "That would be fitting, with the murder weapon being a piece of art."

"They were all art," I hated to point out.

"It does strain credulity that in a fit of passion Mr. Taylor would carefully kill his lover, if she was that, in the same way someone else had killed her sisters so as to divert attention from himself," Mac said.

"Oh," Popcorn said. "Well, that's why you guys are the sleuths. Get sleuthing!"

While Mac ruminated, I cogitated.

"Who among the people on this chart, including the victims, has some kind of link to columbine, rosemary, or violets?" I said finally. (FYI, Oscar's troops had had no joy trying to single out all purchasers of African violets within 50 miles or so of Erin within recent days; no surprise there.)

"*And* violets, old boy," Mac corrected, "not *or* violets. The answer to that, of course, would appear to be the key to unlock the mystery. However, it is a key we do not have."

"Then break a window," Popcorn said. "Hey, wait. That reminds me: No forced entry for any of the three crimes. Who on this list would all the victims open the door for, even after one or two murders?"

"Almost everyone," Mac said, "with the possible exceptions of Gamaliel Taylor in the first two murders and Nathan Daniel in the second two. If the latter victims suspected anyone on this table, they did not say so." He paused, stroked his beard, then dished up: "Perhaps the answer lies in who is not on this chart."

I hate it when he does that.

Popcorn frowned at the computer screen. "This mess is all complicated, not just David Gunner's role."

"It always is," I reminded her.

"What would Nero Wolfe do?" she asked Mac.

"No doubt he would come up with a ruse, a stratagem, or an artifice."

"Why not a scheme, a trick, or a feint?" I asked rhetorically.

Mac got into the spirit of it with, "Or perhaps he would prefer a wile, a maneuver, or a ploy."

For some reason, Popcorn appeared confused.

"In other words," I said, "a trap! Well, we've done that before."

"Indeed we have, old boy," Mac acknowledged. "In those cases,[11] however, we already knew the killer and our stratagems—"

"Or ruses."

"—were designed to prove it."

"This is like watching the sausage being made, and it isn't pretty," my irreplaceable assistant opined. "I'm no detective, but maybe you sleuthhounds should concentrate on the freshest scent."

"The suggestion is not without merit," Mac said. "I spoke to Kate about Desdemona last night. In her opinion, the most unconventional of the Bainbridge sisters was not as, er, 'flaky' as it appeared. She collected art, and artists, with a certain amount of taste. Several emerging artists that she bought early in their careers are now well-known and their paintings valuable. Her penchant for the work of Gamaliel Taylor was a rare lapse, according to Kate. That is a mystery

---

[11] Too many to name!

that may never be solved. Kate suggested, however, that Adam Mendenhall might be persuaded to shed further light on how Mr. Taylor came to be the artist-in-residence at the Shinkle."

The Shinkle Museum of Art is near the river on Front Street, a wonderful old brick and stone building with turrets and towers. In the nineteenth century it was the twenty-room country home of Cincinnati pork baron Nicodemus Shinkle, whose great-granddaughter gifted it to her foundation for use as an art museum.

"I would say I'm glad to see you gentlemen, but I hardly ever do unless there's been a murder."

Adam Mendenhall, who has energetically presided over the Shinkle as director for a dozen years, said all this while pumping our hands. He is a bowtie-and-suspenders kind of guy, about Mac's height (five-ten) and my breadth (reasonably trim, I am, despite the extra COVID pounds, thanks to almost 47 years of healthy eating and regular exercise). We'd once talked to Mendenhall in conjunction with the death of an art critic[12] and had run into him a few other times on the edges of cases.

"We are indeed the stormy petrels of crime," Mac said, sounding tastelessly cheerful about it.

"Sit down and tell me how I can help."

We did so, while Mendenhall left his white kidney-shaped desk to join us in a little grouping of stuffed chairs. The walls around us were covered with paintings, but I knew that none of them were by Gamaliel Taylor because the people in the artwork were clothed.

---

[12] "Art in the Blood," in *Rogues Gallery* (MX Publishing, 2014).

"We were wondering what you can tell us about how Mr. Taylor came to be the first Shinkle artist-in-residence," he said.

Mendenhall's eyes did a Roger Rabbit. I was almost expecting his bowtie (pink, in contrast to Mac's staid blue one with white dots) to spin like a propeller.

"What could that possibly have to do with the murder of the Bainbridge triplets?"

Take your pick: Newcomer in a small town, known womanizer in an ambiguous relationship with one of the victims, artist in a situation where all three murder weapons are works of art, man with easy access to at least one of the victims' homes . . .

At this point in my mental wanderings, I almost called Oscar and asked him to meet us at Taylor's Airstream with handcuffs.

"I have it on good authority," Mac said, meaning both Kate McCabe and Dante Peter O'Neill, "that Mr. Taylor is not a particularly skilled artist, nor at his age can he be said to be showing future promise. That makes his artist-in-residence appointment an anomaly, and anomalies surrounding a murder are always worth further inquiry. In addition, we were told that you initially resisted the appointment by Desdemona Bainbridge's committee."

Mendenhall sighed and fidgeted in his seat, his face almost as pink as his bowtie. It didn't take an expert in body language to see that Mendenhall would rather be the guest of honor at a cannibal picnic than deal with this business. But he manned up, I'll give him that.

"I know you well enough to know you won't let this go," he said. "I presume that everything I tell you will remain among us three?"

"Presuming that our silence would not constitute a crime or immoral act on our part, of course."

That was a loophole big enough to drive a Greyhound bus through, but Mendenhall didn't seem to notice. He nodded and unloaded.

"I'm sure you understand that, although highly regarded, the Shinkle is a very small institution with tenuous funding. We subsist on grants, contributions, admission fees, and memberships. There is no investment by the city, state, or federal government." *Whatever PR genius came up with the idea of calling all government spending "investment" ought to be elected to the Bafflegab Hall of Fame.* "The pandemic shut us down for a while, and then we had to limit attendance. That cut into admission fees, which were not made up for by increased contributions. In short, gentlemen, we were not in a position to turn down the offer of a major contribution by Mrs. Bainbridge, which I was given to understand would come our way if Gamaliel Taylor were the artist-in-residence."

And I thought shenanigans like that only happened in politics and academia.

A McCabe eyebrow jerked upward. "She already funded the artist-in-residence program, did she not?"

"You misunderstand. I said *Mrs.* Bainbridge—that is to say, Mrs. Portia Bainbridge. She has been very generous to many civic projects in town, but never previously to the Shinkle."

"So," Mac said, "by acceding to the relatively harmless appointment of the ungifted Mr. Taylor, you pleased a long-time supporter and secured a new source of funding. I shall not judge you. What will happen now?"

"To the artist-in-residence program, you mean? I'm not sure about the future. That depends on whether someone steps forward to continue funding—Ezra Bainbridge, perhaps. Nothing will change for Taylor. His three-month appointment runs through October 30. As I see it, that is a mercifully brief period. Between now and then he has unique access to the museum with the responsibility to consult, give lectures, and create at least one new work of art. We are under no obligation to display it."

Mendenhall looked miserable, but Mac didn't. I knew what he was thinking.

"You're thinking motive, aren't you?" I said as soon as we were on the museum's front steps.

"Indeed I am, old boy! Surely you have perceived that if there was something untoward between Portia and Mr. Taylor, that would give Arlo Bainbridge a motive for killing his wife?"

"But not to kill her sisters."

"It might—if they knew of her dalliance, and therefore his motive."

"But the sequence is wrong. Why wouldn't he kill Portia first?"

"So that the motive was not so obvious."

"Oh, that again."

Chapter Twenty
The Course of True Love

"Dalliance!" Arlo exclaimed.

We'd found him in his six-car garage, polishing a 1919 Pierce-Arrow roadster. He wore tan shorts and fisherman's sandals, but somehow still looked like the Yale grad that he was.

"He means 'affair,'" I said.

"I know what he means, dammit! It's ridiculous. I'm sure Portia barely knew that slime-ball."

"Why, then, did she so ardently insist that he be the Shinkle's artist-in-residence?" Mac asked.

"Because that was the deal."

"What deal?" I had to ask.

"The deal she made with Des in return for Des supporting her claims of abuse against Fleur. There, I said it! Now will you people leave me alone?"

"At least now we know why Des was on Portia's side in that elder abuse brouhaha," I said that night over dinner with the McCabes at Bobbie McGee's Sports Bar. We'd been making a habit of patronizing the remaining local eateries more than usual to help them recover from the economic ravages of the pandemic.

"How does that help, T.J.?" Kate asked. She would. My big sister never forgets that she's my big sister, never mind that with the same red hair and similar height we could pass for fraternal twins.

"You know Jeff and Mac," Lynda said. She sipped her cocktail. "They love solving mysteries, even minor ones."

"Unfortunately, a very big mystery remains, and it has three heads," Mac said. I had seldom seen him look so gloomy. "We need to re-examine the commonalities among the victims. What did the triplets have in common?"

"They were rich," Kate said.

"They were all hit in the head," Lynda said.

"By an expensive artwork," I added. "Also, they all belonged to WASP and liked to shoot things."

"Just targets," Kate clarified.

"Hey, there's Johanna," Lynda said. She waved at Tall Rawls, who was just entering the crowded restaurant. The leggy reporter, dressed in white shorts showing off a tan that made me worry about her exposure to cancer-causing UV rays, exercised her arm in response. She made her way over to our table.

"Great job on the Bainbridge murder coverage," Lynda praised.

"Thanks. It's a work in progress."

"Hot date?" I asked.

"Medium, I guess." I thought I detected a slight flush in her Nordic face, but maybe I was projecting. Then I remembered I had a dental appointment the next day for my six-month checkup. Tall Rawls's not-so-tall boyfriend, Seth Miller, usually works on my teeth as one of Dr. Marcum's dental technicians.

"I bet you guys are talking about the murders," Johanna said.

"Amazing deduction, Watson," Kate quipped.

"We were in the process of naming what the triplets shared," Mac said.

"You mean like their mother and father and stepmother?"

"Yeah, like that," I said.

"And their family therapist, Mitzi Gold, who told the whole world about their troubles in that book, *Family Lies,*" Kate said.

"They also shared the gardener, Lucius Snedeker, in the sense that he worked for the entire family," Mac mused. "In addition, he was once briefly married to Desdemona, fathered her daughter, and worked closely with Portia on garden matters."

"He used to work here as a waiter years ago," I tossed in, "back when this was Doyle's Irish Pub."

"Their hairdresser!" Lynda said, a note of triumph in her voice. She thumped her cocktail glass on the table. "That's another thing the three victims shared. Myrtle White was their hairdresser and colorist. She mentioned that to me once when she was giving me a French braid. And women tell their colorist things they don't tell anybody else."

The Bainbridge sisters were blondes, like Tall Rawls, except for that streak of violet in Des's hair. But they were 42—maybe they needed help to stay blonde.

"Wait a minute! How would you know what women tell their colorist?" I asked my spouse.

The dark honey color of Lynda Teal Cody's curly tresses doesn't come out of a bottle. I would have noticed.

"I read that in *Shape* magazine," was her throaty response.

Johanna started to laugh, then stopped dead. Buck Melonic was walking toward us, for once not holding his pipe.

"Sorry I'm late," he told Johanna. He kissed her on the cheek. Unlike Seth, he didn't have to stand on his toes to do it.

"That's okay," she said. "We were just catching up."

He gave a boyish grin that seemed a little forced to me. "Will I read about this catching up on page one of the *Observer* tomorrow?"

She shook her head, giving her long, straight hair a workout. "You don't have to worry about that. Mac hasn't solved it yet. But he will."

This was the hometown girl flying the local flag. She was also right, of course.

"I have a few ideas about this case myself," Melonic told Mac, "and I'm following them up. Why let you have all the fun? But I'd like to hear your thoughts. You must have something I can use."

Mac shook his leonine head. "Alas, Mr. Melonic, I am not even certain that I have something that *I* can use."

After exchanging a few platitudes about keeping in touch, the happy couple moved on to their own table in another corner of the restaurant.

"Poor Seth," Kate said, echoing my thoughts.

"He does seem to have taken a back seat in Johanna's affections for the nonce," Mac said. "Perhaps, however, this is simply a passing fancy, the thrill of the new."

"Johanna is flattered by his attentions," Lynda said. "And Buck's closer to her height than Seth and a journalist.

On the other hand, he's a competitor of sorts even though they are collaborating to an extent. And Seth is so sweet."

"You've been talking to Johanna," Kate observed.

"Texting, mostly."

"I didn't know that!" I said.

"I'm sorry, Jeff." Lynda looked adorably contrite. "I didn't think you'd be interested."

I wasn't. But I am now.

"What does she really know about this guy?" I asked.

"She knows quite a bit, actually. She's a reporter, after all." Lynda rattled off the facts. "Buckminster Upton Melonic was born in Pittsburgh 36 years ago to an unmarried mother. Buck never had a father or very much money, but he was bright enough to get a full ride to the University of Cincinnati, where he studied journalism.

"He's had to move around a lot, from one small paper to the next, until he finally landed the position at CNS in Wheeling. Johanna doesn't want to leave Erin, by the way, but she's afraid she might have to if the *Observer* goes down the tubes."

"Is that a real possibility?" Kate asked.

Lynda shrugged. "I hope not, but who knows? The parent company has a lot of debt and sagging revenue."

I thought back to Frank Woodford unloading on that topic in his office, the day we almost ran into Serena Mason coming out of the *Observer* building. She'd been evasive about what she was up to. I made a mental note to look into that. As Lynda said, Mac and I like solving even minor mysteries.

"Every community should have its own newspaper," Mac opined.

"But a lot don't these days," I groused. More than two hundred counties, to be exact, according to a report on "The Expanding News Desert" from the Hussman School of Journalism and Media at the University of North Carolina. I looked that up, too.

"Johanna would make a wonderful TV reporter," Lynda said. "Maybe she could get a job at one of the Cincinnati stations and commute from Erin the way Nadine Lattimore did when she was an anchor at Channel 11."

I glanced over at Tall Rawls and Melonic laughing over drinks, seeming to have a good time, and I remembered their shared contempt for their counterparts in broadcast media.

"I'm not sure she considers that journalism," I said. "What were we talking about before her date showed up?"

"The likelihood that a woman would share secrets with her colorist," Mac said. "I am much intrigued by that."

Chapter Twenty-One
Never Did Run Smooth

"So, did they get all physical right there in front of everybody?" Popcorn demanded.

She was showing more interest that morning in my account of the Rawls-Melonic interaction the night before than in the progress of our murder investigation.

"No, Mac would call them circumspect. Maybe they're friends without benefits."

She gave me a pitying look. I noticed that Rosamund DeLacey's latest romance novel, *Love's Untamed Passion*, lay on her desk. The pseudonymous author had slowed her output in recent years from a flood to a trickle, but Popcorn remained a devoted reader.

This talk about young lovers had me thinking about Goldie and Gunner (she could be Goldie Gunner someday!) and then about my own rather rocky road to love with Lynda, which involved a separation of some months until she proposed. ("I want you to marry me, you neurotic nitwit.")[13]

"What are you smiling about, Boss?"

"Never mind. Get out of here and let me get some work done before my dental appointment this afternoon."

---

[13] See *No Police Like Holmes* (MX Publishing, 2011) and *Holmes Sweet Holmes* (MX Publishing, 2012).

For the next hour I slaved away on a draft news release about Grant Kingsley's big changes for SBU. This was counting chickens before they were hatched, given that the moves needed approval by the trustees, but I wanted to give GK plenty of time to review it.

"I'm counting on Ezra's support, and I need it," he told me over the phone just minutes after I hit the "SEND" button to email him the release. "I've counted the votes. But the man is a basket case mentally, on top of the lingering effects of COVID. He's lost three daughters and he'll never get closure until the murdering bastard is caught."

You can see where this was going, and so could I.

"Mac is working on it," I assured him.

"So I keep hearing."

As an expert on sarcasm, I rated that about one and a half stars.

"I'll keep after him, G.K."

"What's his next move?"

"The Bainbridge sisters' hairdresser, Myrtle White. We're paying her a call after I get finished at the dentist."

"You've known Johanna a long time, right?" Seth Miller asked as he flossed my teeth. I do this myself three times a day, but nobody ever died of over-flossing.

When I could respond, I did: "For some years, sure. Lynda knows her better, of course, being her former boss and mentor."

"Johanna still looks up to Lynda as her role model." I couldn't see Seth's face behind the paper mask, just my own face in his glasses. "She seems a little distracted lately. Johanna, I mean. And not available when I want to go out. And she seems to talk a lot about that Buck Melonic guy, the reporter from Central News Service. If I didn't know better, I'd be jealous. What do you think?"

Incoming! Incoming! I squirmed, at least mentally. If there's a nicer guy on the planet than Seth, I haven't met him. He comes from one of the dozens of Amish families around Erin and is still close to them, although he no longer follows their way of life. If Seth didn't know that Tall Rawls was casting her line in fresh waters, I wasn't going to be the one to tell him. On the other hand, I didn't want to lie.

"Well, she's working hard on covering the Bainbridge murders," I said. This was a fact.

"Yeah. I guess so. She's been writing long stories every day. A sad thing, that. I used to work on Ophelia's teeth. She had excellent gums."

Good to know.

An old theory of mine suddenly sprang back to life, like a zombie. "Did she ever say anything to you about her late husband?" I asked when Seth prepared to switch from flossing to cleaning.

"Not that I can remember. I didn't even know she'd been married."

"He supposedly died during a whitewater rafting accident in Indiana about a dozen years ago." I decided to tell Seth my idea. "It occurred to me after her murder that maybe the husband—one Devan O'Rourke—was still alive and came back to town to kill her. That could still work. Maybe he's out to revenge himself on the whole family."

"They didn't find the body?"

"They"—the ubiquitous "they" sure get around— "did, but it had been in the water so long they had to depend on dental records to identify the body." Now I had to tread carefully. "Dr. Marcum did that, O'Rourke being a patient of this practice. Is there any chance he made a mistake?"

Even through Seth's mask I could tell he had trouble processing that concept.

"I was still in college back then, but I've never known Dr. Marcum to make a mistake. I'm sure he wouldn't make a mistake about something that important. Hey, Kaheesha!"

He was calling to a trim but buxom young woman with dyed yellow curls who was passing in the hall outside the room where I was imprisoned in the dental chair. She halted.

"This is Jeff Cody, Sebastian McCabe's friend." *I prefer to think of Sebastian McCabe as Jeff Cody's friend.* And to me he explained: "Kaheesha is our new technician."

"I love Professor McCabe." *Don't we all?* "I took three of his courses when I was at SBU." She chuckled. "He has such a melonic head. Nice to meet you." She left us to poke into somebody's mouth.

"Melonic head?" I said. "What does that mean?"

"You know, big—as in, melon-like. It's sort of slang, I guess. I've usually heard it applied to, uh, breasts." He stopped. At first, I thought he was embarrassed, and perhaps he was, but he was also in the grip of an idea. "Maybe Melonic isn't that CNS guy's real name. Maybe it's a phony. Maybe *he's* a phony! What do you know about him, Jeff?"

"I know that he's a reporter. And I understand that he had a pretty rocky childhood—Mom wasn't married, and Dad wasn't around. Not much money."

"Gosh, that makes me count my blessings." His brown eyes softened behind the mask. "How do you know all that?"

"I'm a detective. Sebastian McCabe is my Watson."

With flawless timing, the entrance of Dr. Marcum prevented Seth from pressing the point. The good doctor has white hair, and plenty of it. At his age, he's earned it.

"How are you today?" he asked jovially, as medical types often do. That was beyond annoying when I was suffering kidney stone pain at a level of nine on a 1-10 scale, but not so bad during a routine dental visit.

"I'm fine," I assured him. "Do you remember when Devan O'Rourke's body was found . . ."

"First of all, Jefferson, the idea that B.U. Melonic, journalist and would-be amateur sleuth, is using an assumed name is mere speculation," Mac said later that afternoon. "However, even if the speculation is true, that would not necessarily signal evil intentions on his part, as much as I find him an irritant. Perhaps he is disaffected from his family or chose the name 'Melonic' as a statement of grand ambitions, or simply prefers the romance of a pseudonym. I believe your friendship for Seth Miller, and your fear that Mr. Melonic has displaced him in Johanna's affections, is clouding your judgement on this matter."

"Reporters don't use pseudonyms," I snapped. "They're supposed to tell the truth."

Mac nodded his melonic head. "Granted. However, we are getting ahead of ourselves. If all other paths in this case turn out to be of the primrose variety, it would be worth checking the birth records to see if the name Buckminster Upton Melonic is real. That would not be terribly difficult. Such records are online, and we know that he was born in Pittsburgh and he is 36 years old. Or so he told Johanna. Perhaps we shall see. First, however, on to Ms. White."

Myrtle White's downtown Erin salon, Glam Gurlz, survived COVID thanks to her hard work, optimism, and ingenuity. A friendly, upbeat black woman who walks with a limp, she took her hair magic virtual by offering consulting services via Zoom. Lynda and dozens of other women were glad to pay. Now she's back, and two other stylists are renting space from her again. We met with her in a back room.

"How are those kids of yours?" she asked me.

"Oh, you know," I said, "the boys are terrorists and Donata will be in your chair any day now."

"Thank you for your time," Mac told Myrtle.

"It's my lunch hour. But I can't imagine that I know anything helpful about that awful Bainbridge business."

"We understand that you were hairdresser to all three sisters."

She nodded. "Yep. Ophelia just wanted to keep the gray out. Des was making a statement with that streak of violet. Portia got caramel highlights, very sophisticated."

Not exactly what we needed to know, Myrtle.

"Jefferson's premise, based on good authority, is that women share confidences with their hairdresser—eh? very well, then—with their *colorist* that they would not share with mere mortals. Does anything any of the triplets told you seem significant now in light of the murders?"

She thought about that so hard I could almost hear it, then gave her head a sad shake. "Sorry."

"What do you know about them that *doesn't* seem significant?" I asked, desperate. "What did they talk to you about most recently?"

"Des was all wrapped up in this artist, like he was Michelangelo and Andy Warhol all wrapped up in one." *Interesting image.* "I thought maybe they were, you know, but she said not. In fact, she got haughty—almost like Portia—and said she was his patron, not his lover. Des was okay, but she liked to think of herself as a flower child and I think she was secretly guilty about having all that money. She over-tipped.

"Ophelia was the most human of the three, not whacky like Des or stuffy like Portia. She always had something interesting to talk about, whether it was a DNA test she took or using a dating app. She's the one I'll miss."

She paused.

"And that leaves Portia," I prodded.

"Right. Her." Myrtle took a breath. "Portia was a challenge. She'd be a social climber if she wasn't already at the top of the local ladder. Her sisters talked her into trying me after her uptown stylist in Cincinnati messed up so badly that her hair looked like butterscotch. Portia liked my work"—I didn't begrudge Myrtle the note of pride—"but I could tell she had me categorized as 'the help.' All she ever talked about was whatever do-gooder project was going to get her picture in the paper next.

"I don't suppose any of all that helps you."

As it turned out, she was wrong about that.

"Just for the record, and not to overlook the obvious," I said, "can you think of anybody who might want to kill all three for any reason, no matter how wild?"

Myrtle was half-way through a headshake when she stopped. "Have you talked to that therapist, Mitzi Gold? She must have known the triplets better than I did, although I'm not sure she left any secrets untold in that book of hers."

Chapter Twenty-Two
The Lady Doth Protest Too Much

"I thought *Family Lies* was a good title," Mitzi Gold said. "Don't you?"

"It has the virtue of being memorable," Mac conceded.

"And true," Gold said.

This was the first time we'd met her in person, but she looked much the same as when we'd encountered her on a video call during that ghostly murder business at the beginning of the COVID lockdown[14]—short, spikey silver hair and a round face. She wore a white protective mask. We sat in her family relationships counseling office, which was rented space on the second floor of a single-family home on a quiet street not far from downtown. A divorce lawyer held forth downstairs, which I find ironic. But not as ironic as Gold being divorced herself, though still living with ex-husband "Long John" Gold, the pawnbroker. I guess it's complicated.

"That book didn't make you any too popular with some of the oldest money in Erin," I said.

She didn't quite smile beneath her mask. "It's true that a certain family took offense, based on their perception

---

[14] See *No Ghosts Need Apply* (MX Publishing, 2021).

of how they were portrayed in the book, but I've never revealed the names of any individuals whose case histories I discussed in *Family Lies*."

"That was hardly necessary," Mac rumbled, "given that 'Family B' involved a set of triplet women whose mother died at birth. I was told that Desdemona Bainbridge was particularly upset by your characterization of her as a loose cannon liable to self-fire at any time."

"I didn't quite put it that way," Gold said, "but I wish I had. I just gave the facts as part of the backstory of why these three sisters who once shared a womb couldn't share Yankee Stadium until they came to me. Des complained about me to the American Association of Marriage and Family Therapists, but I was far from the first therapist to write about case histories. That goes all the way back to Sigmund Freud. And what would a book on family healing be without them? But I'm grateful to Des. Her dissing me all over Erin and beyond got my name out there. New clients, in person and virtual, are waiting to get in and the book may go into a second printing. I haven't been on Oprah yet, but I did get interviewed for a story on Channel Eleven.

"But, aside from all that, I'm devastated that Ophelia, Portia, and Desdemona are dead, and in such a horrific way. I'm sure you can understand that a therapist gets to know her clients quite well. I suppose I shouldn't even acknowledge that they came to me together for family therapy, but you assured me that this entire conversation is confidential."

Mac nodded assent.

"What exactly did you do for the Bainbridge sisters?" I asked.

"I helped them get past their past."

The big guy looked skeptical. "I have always felt that there is a lot of wisdom in that quote from William Faulkner's novel *Requiem for a Nun*, 'The past is never dead. It's not even past.'" He paused, and then added: "Ophelia Bainbridge was a devotee of Faulkner."

Gold, smartly but simply dressed in a cream-colored blouse and a brown skirt, leaned forward. "Something like one-quarter of the American population is estranged from a close relative at any given time. Lots of times it goes all the way back to childhood—things like 'Mom always liked you best' and 'you stole my boyfriend.' The only way to reconcile is to leave the past and refocus on the present and the future."

"So, who stole whose boyfriend in the Bainbridge family?" I asked. I assumed that Fleur cutting out Portia with Rory Campbell didn't count, never mind that he didn't seem like such a prize anyway.

"You know I can't talk about that," Gold protested.

"Why not? Isn't it in your book? Or are you saving it for your next one?"

She didn't blink under my witty assault. "Suffice it to say that a well-known but emotionally distant father looming in the childhood background, allowing small sibling rivalries to fester into large ones with time, is not an uncommon situation in my practice."

"You encouraged the Bainbridge sisters to engage in a mutual hobby, did you not?" Mac asked.

Gold nodded. "Right. I never expected them to join WASP, but shooting at targets to get rid of their mutual antagonism was better than shooting at each other. The fact that they continued to 'bond over bullets'—as Ophelia called it—after the therapy ended shows that it had value to them, however unconventional."

She pointedly looked at her watch. "I'm no detective, gentlemen, but I don't see how the sisters' relationships with each other could have anything to do with all three of them being murdered. I don't even know why you came here. I think you should follow the money. The Bainbridges have tons of it, and the triplets didn't take theirs with them."

I bet you relieved them of a lot of it when they were in therapy.

"I wonder if she knows that Goldie is Ophelia's heir and presumably Des's as well," I mused to Mac later. "I can't shake the fact that Goldie's alibi is David Gunner, who clearly would like to park his boots under her bed if he isn't already. We never did completely explore my idea that Arlo killed Ophelia and Des, in return for Goldie killing Portia."

"You persist in that? How do you account for the flowers left at each murder?"

"Well, that's still a puzzler. If they were a dying message, Ophelia's yellow flowers could have been pointing to Goldie—columbine because marigolds weren't handy."

"But they were, old boy."

"Eh?"

"Did you fail to notice the vase of marigolds on an end table in a corner of the room not ten feet from Ophelia's body? They would have been the perfect dying message from Ophelia the mystery reader had Marigold Bainbridge killed her. Except, of course, under your scenario it would have been Arlo and not Goldie who executed the murder. Also, we now know that it is the killer who has this mysterious habit of leaving flowers at the scene."

See why this stuff gives me headaches?

"Ms. Gold's rather hackneyed observation about the possibility of a money motive does give me pause, however," Mac steamed on. "Wealthy families often have rather complex trusts to pass on wealth to the next generation, favorite charities, and the like. The ultimate beneficiary of these three murders may be someone or some institution that we would not expect. We should visit David Gunner on Monday. I suspect he could enlighten us on the Bainbridge arrangements along those lines."

"I'm sure he could! Estate planning is one of his firm's specialties. But that doesn't mean he would. Lawyers have that pesky client confidentiality thing."

"So do therapists, old boy."

He had me there, but I had another thought.

"Maybe following the money should take us to Gunner, not as Goldie's accomplice but on his own behalf. Being the attorney for an old-money family might provide opportunities for financial shenanigans on his part. They probably don't keep as close an eye on their greenbacks as the people who earned the stuff. So maybe Gunner was dipping into the till and the sisters found out."

Mac's objection was immediate. "All theories in this case that hypothesize murder to prevent exposure suffer from the same weakness: Why kill Ophelia, Portia, and Desdemona several days apart? Looked at as a family tragedy, their deaths were close together. Looked at as a way of eliminating threats to the killer, they were far apart. If they all had the same guilty knowledge about someone, Ophelia's murder would have strengthened her sisters' resolve to expose the miscreant immediately."

"Maybe the other two only came to that knowledge after her murder."

"Surely, Jefferson, the killer would have acted earlier if he even suspected that was a possibility."

Lynda seemed more enthusiastic when I told her my idea at cocktail hour.

"That's quite clever, darling!" she said.

"You think Mac's pushback was wrong?"

"No, but I still think your theory is clever. Who would suspect David Gunner? He's adorable! Oh, don't get that look on your face. Aside from being eye candy, he's adorable the way a puppy dog is adorable. I hope Goldie doesn't take him for granted."

The kids were being quiet, Lynda was comfortably dressed in a red-yellow-and-blue flowered caftan after taking a pre-dinner shower, and I was feeling mellow. So why was I talking about the Stratford Court murders? Because Lynda wanted to, and I didn't need a family counselor to tell me I should cooperate. She'd been home with the kids all day, and I was bringing the outside world to her. When I got to the part where I quoted Seth Miller talking about the urban-dictionary word "melonic" being applied to "um, breasts," could I help it if my eyes wandered? Bearing three children has not caused the sands of Lynda's hourglass figure to shift significantly.

"Poor Seth," Lynda said. "I'm not sure how serious Johanna is about Buck Melonic—she probably doesn't know herself—but she's been spending a lot of time with him on and off the job. That means less time with Seth. Whether he knows it consciously or not, he'd love Buck Melonic to be some kind of fake."

Chapter Twenty-Three
Best Beware My Sting

Lynda and Triple M (AKA Sister Polly) took the kids to the Cincinnati Zoo on Saturday while I worked at home. Wearing khakis and sneakers, I did some preliminary editing on the SBU alumni mag *Ben* to soothe my troubled conscience about spending so much company time on the Stratford Court business. Since my home office on our screened-in porch is where I worked from home during the lockdown months of 2020 and earlier in 2021, this was like *déjà vu* all over again, as a great philosopher said.

"Polly and I were talking about your case," Lynda announced when she returned.

Sister Sherlock!

"How'd that work out?"

She bit her lip in thought. "See what you think of this: Since the killer went to the unnecessary trouble of buying violets, apparently not knowing they are as common as dandelions in Erin, I say we should investigate the out-of-towners."

I didn't have the heart to tell her I'd had some thoughts along those lines myself. "What do you mean, 'investigate'?"

"While the kids nap tomorrow, I'll take a little detour from writing my novel to do some internet research and see what I can dig up on Gamaliel Taylor and Buck Melonic."

"Melonic!"

"There is that question as to whether he is who he says he is. Mac hasn't followed up on that, has he?"

"Not that I know of. This wouldn't have anything to do with you being worried about Johanna being romanced by this guy, would it?"

"Don't be silly, darling."

As it happened, Lynda never got to her laptop for research on Sunday. Between church and an unexpected playdate, there was no time for it. And by the time the kids were down for the count, so were we.

"Any breakthroughs?" Popcorn asked when she brought me my decaf on Monday morning.

"The investigation is ongoing," I assured her. "Did you ask Oscar that, or were you too busy canoodling all weekend?"

Sitting down, she ignored the second part of the question. "Oscar's troops have done all the things that cops do—questioned the housemates, parents, spouses, and children of the victims; sent all the physical evidence to the BCI;[15] canvassed all the neighbors. His overtime bill is going through the roof with nothing to show for it."

"He must be very tense, poor guy. You should help him with that."

"Stop it. Oscar is so desperate he admits he needs Mac to solve this."

"That must be why he's calling the big guy every few hours. How's the intern working out?"

"She's a keeper!"

---

[15] Ohio Bureau of Criminal Investigation, the state's crime lab.

What with one thing and another—another being a national media call for a survey story about colleges and universities using technology to keep tabs on students (*who, us?*)—it was late morning before I called Mac to press him about talking to David Gunner.

"You think you can crack his lawyerly reserve and get him to dish about the Bainbridges," I reminded him, "and I still think he's a suspect, no matter how adorable Lynda thinks he is."

"Lynda?"

"Never mind."

Within a few minutes, we were on our way in Mac's land yacht to the Bridges Law Firm on Market Street. Or so I thought. Mac took a slight detour to The Bull's Eye Gun Shop & Shooting Range, unannounced.

"This is no time to be playing with your .32," I told him when we pulled up in front.

"I quite agree, nor is that my intention," he huffed as he unbuckled his seatbelt. The lack of discernable progress in this case had made him a little testy. "You yourself noted that one of the commonalities among the three victims was that they were all members of WASP."

Hoisted by my own petard! Whatever a petard is.

Remind me to have the marketing types at SBU cast Grady Sanders as a professor in their next online ad. The manager of The Bull's Eye is perfect for the part, with snow white hair where he isn't bald on top, an equally white full beard, big glasses, and a mouthful of large teeth not covered by a mask. Mac knew him well, being a habitué of his establishment, but this was my first encounter although I'd been to the range a few times.

After letting Sanders express shock and grief at the murders, Mac asked what he knew about the triplets.

"Not much. Just that they were Bainbridges and members of WASP, which kind of gave me a kick. They didn't chat with me a lot, you know? Sometimes they raised their voices at each other a little on the way to the range. But who doesn't have words now and then with their siblings? Besides, a lot of those WASP ladies have a bit of a sting, if you know what I mean."

"What did they argue about?" Mac asked.

"I don't eavesdrop on my customers. In fact, I make a point of that."

"Quite admirable of you, to be sure! At any rate, what divided the three sisters is less likely to relate to their murders than what united them. Presuming they were all killed for the same motive, that is."

"A good sleuth presumes nothing," I informed my brother-in-law.

"I know two things the Bainbridge triplets had in common," Sanders said.

"And that would be?" Mac asked.

"Their mother and their father."

When we got to Gunner's office, he hadn't clocked in yet. (My grandfather used to talk about "banker's hours," but in my experience, lawyers have it even better). Nor was Goldie on the scene—the receptionist informed us she was taking bereavement time off.

But the legendary James Hancock Bridges, he of the thick gray mustache and short-sleeved shirt, saw us in the reception area and waved us into his well-appointed office. We knew him in part because he'd once done a turn on the

SBU board, as he had on almost every volunteer board in town. He knew everybody and, therefore, almost everything. When Jim Bridges was in a talking mood, it paid to listen.

"I'm devastated by the Bainbridge murders," he said, shaking his head as we sat in the offered chairs. "I remember when those girls were born."

I realized then that Bridges must have been a near-contemporary of Ezra, somewhere in his mid- to late-seventies, although far more vigorous than the Bainbridge patriarch.

"What was their mother like?" Mac asked. "Ophelia said that she was an artist."

"Juliet?" Bridges leaned back, a wan smile on his face. "Yes, she painted watercolors and exhibited in local art shows. I'd forgotten that. She was a beautiful woman, like her daughters. Quite a bit younger than Ezra—ten or twelve years, as I recall. She was an Alcott, so her family had status in town, but not a lot of real money. Generations of big spenders took care of that. In any other family, Juliet would have been a black sheep. She liked to party. It was a bit of a surprise when she finally settled down and married Ezra."

"How did that come to be?"

Bridges shrugged his shoulders. "I'm sure there was gossip at the time that money was part of the equation. Maybe that's true, and maybe it's not. Maybe it's partly true. Who knows? But they were married a few years by the time she got pregnant, long enough for her to change her mind about being Mrs. Bainbridge if she wanted to."

"And walk away with a pile of money under a pre-nuptial agreement, you mean?" That was me, adding two and two out loud.

Bridges smiled. "Now you're getting into a question to which I actually know the answer, but I can't tell you because of attorney-client privilege."

"I guess you also can't tell us who benefits most financially from the sisters' deaths, even though some of it eventually will be a matter of public record," I said.

"That's not really a guess, Jeff. And don't waste your time sniffing around David. How's the new academic year going?"

We were barely out of Jim Bridges's office before Mac fired up a cigar, signaling that the McCabe brain synapses were also firing up.

"Why the question about Juliet Bainbridge?" I asked.

He thoughtfully blew smoke upward. "Because, old boy, I cannot escape my conviction that Faulkner was right: the past is not past."

"What, precisely, does that mean in this particular context, as opposed to a seventy-year-old novel?"

"How I wish I knew!"

"McCabe!" David Gunner was heading our way, talking as he walked. He was dressed in what passes for business casual in the legal world, a blue blazer with tan slacks and no tie. At least he didn't have a carefully cultivated three-day growth of beard. "Please tell me you've made some progress."

He can tell you that, but it won't be true.

"Sometimes progress can be hard to measure," Mac temporized.

"I just came from Stratford Court," Gunner said, "and a damned good thing I was there. I had to chase away a wire service reporter."

"Close to my height with scruffy, blond whiskers?" I asked.

"That's him."

"Ah, Mr. Melonic," Mac said. "He fancies himself something of an amateur sleuth in competition with yours truly."

Gunner wasted no time on that. "Whatever. I met him at the door. He wanted to talk to Ezra or, failing that, anybody in the house. I told him 'no way.' I reminded the guy in strong terms that he was trespassing, and that the property owners were within their rights to forcibly remove him." He grinned at the memory. "I think Goldie was impressed. She was in the house with her grandfather. This is tearing her up. She was close to her aunts, especially Ophelia, and she loved her mom even though they didn't always see eye to eye."

"Maybe that's the point," I blurted. The idea just popped out, without consulting me first.

"What do you mean?" Gunner asked.

"Maybe the killer wants to hurt Goldie."

He looked at me like I had two heads, spinning in opposite directions. "That's so far-fetched it's off the charts. You should write fiction, Cody." *Believe me, I've tried.* "Everybody loves Goldie."

"Aren't you speaking for yourself?"

He reddened. "None of your business." He was more shouting than speaking now. "What's between Goldie and me is between Goldie and me."

Well, I can't deny that.

"If one were to pursue Jefferson's rather implausible and even fanciful line of thought," Mac mused, looking at his cigar with affection, "Ezra Bainbridge would seem to be even more of a victim of these heinous murders."

"I'm not sure there is an Ezra anymore, in any real sense," Gunner said. "He was already having a lot of brain fog because of long COVID, and now he's lost all three daughters in a little more than a week. Maybe he wasn't exactly a soccer dad, or the one who was there at all the Hallmark moments, but I'm sure he loved them. It's painful for me to watch. I've known him all my life and he was vigorous up until about a year ago. Now he sits huddled in that wheelchair."

"Is he really that far gone?" I asked.

"In and out, but mostly out." I made a mental note to tell GK he might soon have one less SBU board member to convince about his big plans.

"Mrs. Bainbridge told me that he seemed uncomprehending after Portia's death," Mac said. "Since then, I have been unwilling to intrude upon the family grief any more than necessary."

"I couldn't say it's gotten any worse, in a sense. I mean, how much worse than two deaths is three? How do you quantify that? At some point, the grief reflex must shut down. But Fleur tries to shield Ezra from the news accounts. She hides the newspaper from him. When he asked for it yesterday while I was there, she handed him the sports section." The Sunday *Observer* had a story by veteran editor-writer Ben Silverstein recapping the importance of the Bainbridge family in the history of Erin, going back to riverboat days. "It's touching the way she takes care of him. They could well afford a private nurse, but she does it all."

"A cynic might think she didn't want to have a third party on the scene 24/7, especially a nurse," I said. *And I'm a cynic.*

"Some people think too much."

"Maybe, but the opposite seems more of a problem these days."

Mac studied his cigar. "Your reference to the Bainbridge fortune, Mr. Gunner, does make one wonder what will happen to it when Ezra Bainbridge, weakened from illness and this series of tragedies, passes from the scene."

"Keep wondering."

I still didn't find David Gunner adorable, but I was starting to like his style.

"Your professional ethics are admirable, Mr. Gunner. However, this is a murder investigation."

"And you're not the police, who might conceivably have a right to ask questions that are none of your business."

"Touché! However, we have been asked by Ezra Bainbridge himself to investigate."

"Then you can ask him, in turn, anything you want to know about family finances. If you can get him to understand you and answer." Gunner sighed in a way that made me think he was tired of sparring. Maybe he was up late with Goldie last night, not sparring. "Look, I don't want to be a butthead about this. And I don't want you to waste a lot of time going off on a false premise. I think it would be permissible for me to make the general statement that Ezra has set up a very sophisticated arrangement of wills and trusts to provide for various non-profits that are important to him."

I hope he has SBU covered.

That got a raise out of a McCabe eyebrow. "Non-profits? What about family members?"

"Well, Fleur benefits, of course. Under Ohio state law, a spouse inherits at least as much as he or she would if the deceased died intestate. In other words, Ezra couldn't disinherit her if he wanted to. Not that he wanted to. And, of course, he set up a trust for the three grandchildren—Goldie and Portia's two kids, Astrid and Harley. Lot of females in that family!"

Goldie again!

"And the three daughters, if they had not died first?"

"Ezra settled substantial sums on them when he married, using something called a Crummey trust in order to avoid gift taxes." Gunner winced, not adorably. "I'm not sure I should have told you that. But I heard Ezra tell Ralph Pendergast at a party once, so he apparently didn't consider it a secret."

For a guy who couldn't talk about clients, he'd spilled a lot. Was that the result of a leaky mouth, or by design? I made a mental note to wonder about that later.

"Avoiding gift taxes doesn't sound like a crummy idea to me," I observed.

He spelled it out. "Gulliver Mackie suggested it. He's been Ezra's financial advisor for years. Do you know him?"

"Well enough to pay him a visit," Mac said. "And I think we shall do so posthaste."

Chapter Twenty-Four
Outrageous Fortune

Real money whispers because it doesn't need to shout. Gulliver Mackie's wealth management firm operates out of a 1950s Cape Cod house on the edge of downtown Erin without a sign out front. From there, with the aid of one personal assistant, he manages the investment portfolios of Erin's wealthiest families—even the Gambles—but also some of the one percent in Cincinnati, Louisville, and environs. He also owns a big chunk of our business district.

Mackie and my boss, Lesley Saylor-Mackie, form a handsome and distinguished couple in their mid-sixties. (If either one ever had a gray hair out of place, I never saw it.) That's why he said:

"I appreciate that you two have a special interest in the Bainbridge murders because of Ezra's position on the SBU board. But I'm sure you realize that I can only talk about the family's financial position in the vaguest terms."

"Of course," Mac said.

"Well, then, Ezra and Fleur Bainbridge and the triplets are all my clients. That's all you need to know."

Translation: If they didn't have gobs of money, they wouldn't be my clients. I've heard that Mackie might handle a mere half-million-dollar portfolio, but only if the client was still in the accumulation stage. I'll stick with my stock and bond index funds, with the asset allocation rebalanced yearly.

"Is all of the Bainbridge family wealth under your management?" Mac asked.

Mackie frowned. "Not quite. Desdemona Bainbridge declined to treat her art collection as the financial asset it was. As a result, she was overweighted in art. In addition to increasing her financial risk, that created liquidity problem for her—she could have used more cash. I'm not an art advisor, but I gave her a referral to one and some general advice about art as an investment, both of which she ignored."

"Advice such as?"

"The works of her friend Gamaliel Taylor are quite valuable right now, as part of a general rise in the price of American paintings. That's because the U.S. stock market is soaring. Since American paintings are mostly bought by Americans, their value tends to fluctuate with U.S. equities. When equities are down, Americans have less money to spend on American paintings. But now they're up. I advised Des that this might be a good time to sell."

"And her reaction?"

"I try not to use that kind of language. Arlo Bainbridge is in something of a similar situation with his car collection, which is another illiquid investment. Like all commodities, the values of classic cars have shot up over the past year, which could seriously affect his asset allocation. But I'm just a spectator in that situation. Arlo also has another financial advisor, Brad Thompson of Louisville, who has advised his branch of the Bainbridge family for many years."

It's not unusual for big money to split the pot. My pot isn't big enough for that. But all this talk of classic cars had me wondering how much my 1998 New Beetle is worth. Probably not as much as Lynda's Mustang.

"Frank Woodford told us that Arlo does a little day trading," I reported. "His exact word was 'dabbles.'"

Mackie grimaced. "I'm aware of that from Portia. It's not a course I would advise."

"Day trading" is jumping in and out of a stock during the course of a day for quick profits. At least, that's the goal. It's the opposite of buying stocks or mutual funds for the long haul, what I think of as "patient money." The Robinhood mobile app has made it easy for small investors to play the day trading game. And it is a game, for some.

"So, did he lose a lot of money?" I asked.

"On the contrary. Since he's not my client, I feel free to tell you my understanding is that he made a small fortune on GameStop by getting in and getting out at the right time, probably by sheer luck that is not likely to be enjoyed again."

GameStop's shares skyrocketed 1,500 percent over two weeks in late January 2021 because of a short squeeze by social media users pushing up the price. It didn't last.

"Old money makes new money," I quipped.

"If Portia Bainbridge's murder were the only one," Mac said, "we doubtless would be looking closely at her husband. From what you tell us, however, he would seem to have no financial motive."

"Or any other, if you want my opinion," Mackie said. "They seemed a solid couple. If Arlo has a mistress, she has four wheels and a hood ornament."

"Well, here we are up a creek without a canoe," I said back in Mac's car.

"Would you care to expound on that, old boy?"

"We've spent the last two hours running the money trail only to find out that nobody has a money motive," I reminded him. "Ezra has already given his daughters their inheritance. That means that when Fleur eventually inherits, she gets no more with them gone than if they were alive. Ditto for the three grandchildren. Arlo has his own pile of Bainbridge money, plus his investment gains; you don't even have to count the soaring value of his cars. Goldie inherits from the first and third victim, but we already knew that."

At this point I realized that Sebastian McCabe was staring straight ahead, not starting the car.

"What did I say?" I asked.

"You said, 'Ezra has already given his daughters their inheritance.' Suppose his spouse, who by all accounts is an affectionate wife and attentive caregiver, nonetheless has come to resent that fact. Suppose that Mrs. Bainbridge holds an extreme animus against her stepdaughters that began with the inheritance and was exacerbated by Portia's accusation against her. That would explain the violence of their deaths."

"But Ophelia defended Fleur," I objected. "She even came to you to help."

"Mrs. Bainbridge may have resented all the more being defended by one of the women who deprived her of wealth she thought should belong to her."

"Where do the flowers fit in?"

After a pause, Mac looked at me. "Ophelia told us that the late Juliet Bainbridge liked to paint watercolors of flowers. Perhaps those paintings included a columbine, rosemary, and African violets. I believe it is time for us to make another visit to Stratford Court."

Chapter Twenty-Five
The Envious Court

On our way to the Bainbridge compound, I fielded two phone calls, five e-mails, and three texts that had backed up while we were getting the lowdown on the triplets' family finances. I was so busy I didn't realize until later that it was past lunch time, and I was hungry. One of the texts was from Lynda. Just as we pulled into the cul-de-sac known as Stratford Court, with its English garden somehow looking sad in the light of the three murders, I read:

hot on the melonic trail! luv you ♥

"Mr. Melonic!" Mac bellowed.

Before I could upbraid him for reading my text, I realized that he wasn't talking to me. Buck Melonic was leaning against a wrought-iron lamppost, an architectural nicety not common in Erin, smoking his curved pipe. He waved in response to Mac's hail, and we exited the Chevy.

"I am surprised to see you here," Mac told the journalist. "Mr. Gunner informed us that he removed you from Ezra Bainbridge's property with some vigor."

"You could say that," the reporter acknowledged. "That guy is tougher than he looks. I've been thrown out of bars with more delicacy. But he can't touch me now, legally. I'm standing on a public sidewalk."

"To what end?"

"I want to see who comes calling, maybe catch an interview. So—" He pressed "record" and held out his phone. "—what have you learned?"

"What have you?" Mac countered.

"I asked first."

Show me yours and I'll show you mine. After a little more bantering, Melonic realized that Mac was going to play the Sphynx until he showed his hand.

"My instincts tell me that in some way the family patriarch, Ezra Bainbridge, is the key to this whole mess," he said. "After all, he's one thing the three murder victims had in common. So I've been researching him. There's a great story there—the inherited millions, the Shakespeare fixation that even extends to the names of his first wife and his children, the death of Juliet during childbirth, the hard-charging civic activism as if to make meaning out of his pampered life, and now the long COVID that has him confused and in a wheelchair, topped by the murder of his three daughters. It's almost a Shakespearean tragedy."

"That's one way of looking at it," I said. "But Ezra's no Macbeth."

"I wonder. Now it's your turn, McCabe. Give!"

"We have all but eliminated the traditional motives of love and money, based on our interviews with those closest to the victims and with their legal and financial advisors."

"So what brings you here, then?"

"A notion that came to me a short time ago, based on a different motive. It would be premature to share it, lest I be guilty of the sin of calumny if I am in error."

The man can really pile it on at a moment's notice, I have to admit that. But Melonic was unimpressed. He expressed the opinion that Mac's response was bovine excrement, or a word to that effect.

"And I'm going to say so in my story," he added. "The lead sentence will be something like, 'Mystery writer and amateur sleuth Sebastian McCabe is clueless in the horrific murders of three wealthy sisters.'"

Mac cocked an eyebrow. "That is inaccurate, and you know it. We are not without clues or theories. What we are lacking is the certainty that would give me the confidence to share my theory with you."

Melonic saw it then. "And that's why you're here—to kick the tires on said theory."

"Colorfully put, but essentially correct."

"I can't even get my foot in the door of Ezra Bainbridge's mini-mansion."

"Too bad," I said. "It might be amusing to see Goldie slam the door on it."

"She left about half an hour ago," Melonic reported. "If you're going in there, why not let me tag along?"

"To what end?

"The public's right to know." *The last refuge of journalists and other scoundrels!* "Don't you want me to be there when you pull a rabbit out of your hat?"

Maybe Melonic had been reading my books after all.

"I am not even certain that I have a hat," Mac said. "And if I do, it might be empty."

Please stop these extended metaphors before somebody gets hurt.

"We can put this on an off-the-record basis," Melonic said. "Let me go in with you and I won't report what happens until the case is closed. I won't even ask questions. You'll barely know that I'm there."

I snorted.

"I am reluctant," Mac said.

"You'd do it for Johanna." Melonic's tone was wheedling.

"I know and trust Ms. Rawls."

"Since you brought up Johanna," I said, "she's local, she's our friend, and if we were going to give any reporter the inside track it would be her."

"I've been giving Johanna whatever I've got." *I bet!* "After all, we're not competitors in the business sense. Her newspaper subscribes to the Central News Service."

Mac surrendered with a sigh. "I very much fear that I may regret this."

The young woman who opened the door wore apprehension on her face like makeup, as if she were poised to take life's latest blow. Or maybe she just needed sleep. She had dark hair gathered in a ponytail, blue eyes, and a slim figure accented by her pencil skirt. I didn't need Sebastian McCabe's powers of deduction to tell me that this was Nicole Anderson, the single mom suborned by Portia Bainbridge into letting her poke into Fleur's effects looking for dirt.

"Yes?"

"Good day." If Mac had a hat, he would have doffed it. "Please tell Mrs. Bainbridge that Sebastian McCabe and friends are here to pay a courtesy call on her and on Mr. Bainbridge, if he is up to visitors."

"Just a minute."

It was more like five minutes before she came back and asked us to wait in the library. We had barely seated ourselves in the large room before Melonic picked an all-too-familiar volume off the coffee table.

"Here's that book on the language of flowers that you told me about," he said to me, holding up Monica Porlock's *A Rose by Any Other Name.* "I downloaded a copy. The flowers look brilliant on my tablet."

"In three murders surrounded by flowers, no roses," I pointed out, addressing Mac. "Rosemary, but not roses. And it's one of the most familiar of all flowers, which is probably why your friend Dr. Porlock picked up that particular Shakespeare quote for the title of her book. So, why not a rose in this case?"

"An astute question, Jefferson! Presumably a rose would not convey whatever message the killer wishes to send us. The flower has been associated with love since the ancient Greeks, you will recall." He'd already lectured me on that in the same room the day we went there with Ophelia, which seemed long ago.

"If you're saying the killer didn't love his victims, that makes sense," Melonic said.

Is that sarcasm? I can't tell.

Mac drummed his fingers against the armrest of the chair. "Columbine, rosemary, violets. Of all the possible meanings of those flowers, what do they mean to the killer?"

"Hello, Sebastian, Jeff. Thanks for coming. Ezra is in no shape to see anyone, as I'm sure you'll understand."

We all looked toward the doorway. The Cody brain couldn't help registering that even in the current strained circumstances Fleur Bainbridge remained a striking woman, with attractive features and a body kept trim by years of tennis and bicycling. She moved toward us with grace and elegance. We all stood as one.

And then she frowned.

"Isn't that Mr. Melonic? I was under the impression that our attorney made it clear his presence in Stratford Court is unwelcome."

Talking about Melonic and not *to* him was a nice touch, I thought. Melonic opened his mouth to say something, but Mac saved him from himself.

"You are not mistaken on either count," he told Fleur. "I apologize for this breech of hospitality on my part. Mr. Melonic and I have reached an understanding that should render him harmless."

Thus reminded of his deal, Melonic fumed quietly.

"It hardly matters, really," Fleur said. "What can the media do to what's left of this family compared to what some nameless monster has already done? And he's still out there. What next? *What next?*"

"I regret with all my heart that I was unable to find the culprit after Ophelia's murder," Mac said. "And I assure you that I have not given up."

If Fleur were the killer, she would read that as a threat. But as far as I could tell, she took it as a promise.

"Thank you. What lines are you pursuing?"

For a big man, Mac can dance with some dexterity around a topic.

"At the moment we are looking at who had possible motives," he said truthfully, "and trying to make sense of the various flowers left at the scene of each murder."

"Didn't Ezra's first wife paint watercolors of flowers?" I asked.

"Juliet? Yes, she did. How did you know?"

"Ophelia mentioned it. Did Juliet happen to paint columbines, rosemary, and violets?"

"The death flowers? What could that possibly have to do—" The second Mrs. Bainbridge shook her head. "No, she only did marigolds, her favorite flower. It was just a hobby. From what I've heard, she must have painted dozens of them and given them away to friends. She made some of them into individually painted notecards. Like this one."

Fleur went over to one of the bookshelves and pulled down a small frame. The watercolor inside seemed nicely done, to my unartistic eye. It reminded me of the tattoo on Desdemona Bainbridge's chest.

"The girls grew up knowing about their mother's affection for this particular flower," Fleur said. "That's where Goldie's name came from. And the garden outside started with marigolds."

"'The marigold, that goes to bed with the sun,'" Mac quoted.

"That's from *The Winter's Tale*, isn't it?" Fleur said, not really a question. The Cody memory banks kicked in that she'd met Ezra at a performance of *Macbeth*.

"Indeed."[16]

"Shakespeare seems to be all over this case," Melonic butted in. So much for his vow of monkish silence.

"I'm pretty sure we can connect almost anything to Shakespeare if we try hard enough," I fired back. The devil needed an advocate, and it looked like I was elected. Besides, Melonic annoyed me.

"But the 'death flowers,' as she called them—"

Mac silenced the reporter with a look that could, if not kill, at least seriously maim. Then he turned his attention back to Fleur.

---

[16] Act IV, Scene 3—*S.McC.*

"Your husband has a photograph of his first wife here in this room in which he undoubtedly spends so much time with his books." He nodded toward the framed photo on the library table, which he'd noted in our previous visit. "And he has her artwork here as well. Do you resent her?"

Fleur seemed to suddenly realize that she had the watercolor in her hand. She put it back on the shelf, responding as she did so. "Resent? Don't be ridiculous, Sebastian. The woman has been dead for more than forty years, most of my life. What are you getting at?"

"I am trying to get at the truth. If you did not resent your predecessor, did you harbor such feelings toward the triplets who could never regard you as their mother, who were given a good portion of your husband's wealth, and the majority of whom accused you of elder abuse?"

Fleur blanched. Her hands tightened into fists. "Get out of this house. Right now."

Mac didn't blink. "That is an understandable, and expected, response. However, when your husband asked me to investigate Ophelia's murder, he placed no restrictions upon me. I would appreciate an answer."

I could have counted to at least five while she figured out how to respond.

"All right then," she said finally. "I'll talk to you in deference to your friendship with Ezra, but he"—she nodded toward Melonic—"has to go."

"Hey!" the journalist objected.

"And if you don't," she addressed him directly, "I will call the police and charge you with trespassing."

Melonic opened his mouth as if to protest, then closed it and stalked out of the room.

"I apologize for bringing him," Mac said. "That was, perhaps, an error on my part."

"There's no 'perhaps' about it. It's also an error on your part to be interrogating me."

"I would not characterize my questions as such. I am pursuing a line of inquiry where it takes me. So far you have done nothing to make me think that I should withdraw those questions."

Fleur relaxed a bit, letting her fists fall away. "The inheritance part never disturbed me. Ezra made the situation clear before we married. Besides, unlike Juliet, I brought a substantial amount of my own money into the marriage. Gulliver Mackie can verify that, if necessary. I will give him permission. But it bothered me deeply that Portia and Des never gave me a chance. Only Ophelia was decent to me. But I tried to love them all the same because their father loved them, and I love their father."

"And yet," Mac said, "you kept the love letters from your first husband."

She showed no surprise at our knowledge of this, probably having figured it was part of the dirty laundry that Ophelia hung out in front of us when she asked Mac to help.

"Yes—yes I did, and for one reason only: I wanted to remind myself how foolish I was to marry him. Nobody forced me into it; it was my own bad decision. I should have seen past the medical degree into the bad character that was Rory Campbell—the drinking, the philandering."

Mac nodded, and I wondered if that meant he bought the explanation. "To get back to your stepdaughters, one of them accused you of neglecting and abusing your husband, and the other supported her."

"That did not escape the attention of the police," she said dryly. "The assistant chief, Colonel Gibbons, questioned me at some length about it after Portia's death—including my alibi."

"You had one?" I asked. "Just for the record."

"By a strange fluke, I did. I spend most of my time here looking after Ezra, which Portia accused me of not doing. But I was volunteering at Serenity House during the time Arlo was absent from their home on the day of the murder. Nicole was here and could if Ezra needed me."

"How do you know when Arlo was absent?"

"Colonel Gibbons told me."

"No doubt you can understand his interest in you," Mac said, "given the dead woman's allegations of spousal neglect and more."

"I wasn't worried about Portia's charges in the least. Ezra's old friend Dr. Abington will testify that I make sure my husband gets the best of care, and that he's therefore likely to live a good many years longer despite the long COVID. If the murder of his daughters doesn't kill him. He's a broken man, Sebastian."

Chapter Twenty-Six
What's in a Name?

"So," I said over a very late lunch at an almost-empty Daniel's Apothecary, "did you find her convincing?"

"Eminently so," Mac replied, digging into a heart-attack inducing burger known as the Big Bopper.

"Well, I still like money motives," I said, "and the only person who had one was Goldie."

"Not quite, old boy. You forget Astrid and Harley, the offspring of Portia Bainbridge Bainbridge. One could envision a remote possibility that they are eager to inherit from their mother."

"Their father would inherit from their mother," I pointed out. "Although, I suppose in that case he might have a short life-span under your scenario."

"This is nuts," Buck Melonic objected. He'd attached himself to us upon our departure from Ezra's manse, rather like a leech, and pried out of Mac a summary of what he'd missed from Fleur Bainbridge. "Those kids are at Dartmouth. The killer's flowers-on-the-corpses business smacks of some kind of language-of-flowers message. No college student would do that."

"On the contrary, Mr. Melonic, that is exactly the sort of thing a college student newly inebriated by Shakespeare might do. There is a certain immaturity to it." Melonic turned red beneath his wispy blond beard. "However, I was merely engaging in an intellectual exercise. If the grandchildren had a lust for inherited wealth and a murderous impulse to acquire it, it would be far more direct for them to kill Ezra Bainbridge. Surely they know that he has provided for them with trust funds."

Sipping my Caffeine-Free Diet Coke, I enjoyed their verbal jousting.

"You know," Melonic said, with the air of one going slightly off-topic, "if Ophelia weren't dead, she could be a suspect herself, with the shades of Shakespeare in these murders and her being an English prof."

Mac dismissed that with a headshake. "The Bard was far from Ophelia's passion. Her father, by contrast—"

Mac's phone rang. Instead of a jovial "Sebastian McCabe here!" he answered with, "Hello, Johanna." Melonic brightened up. "Yes, we have made a great deal of progress in eliminating not only the impossible but also the improbable. That is not for publication, and I am not sure that it will help you very much. Mr. Melonic seems frustrated. Yes, he is—"

At this point, *my* phone rang. Not wanting an audience, I left the table to take a call from Seth Miller.

"Hi, Jeff. Just wondering what you found out about that Melonic guy. If his name *is* Melonic."

I looked across the room at Melonic, who was looking at Mac, who was talking to Johanna.

"Lynda's looking into it," I assured him. "I'll get back to you on that."

"Thanks. I had dinner with Johanna last night, but she seemed distracted. I don't know whether she had her mind on him or on worries about her job. She said there's some big announcement coming from corporate on Friday and she's afraid it might be layoffs or, even worse, a sale to one of those big media companies that fires everybody."

"Sounds grim. It's your job to comfort her, Seth."

"I wish I could."

"Buckminster Upton Melonic's real name is"— *dramatic pause*—"Buckminster Upton Melonic," Lynda informed me over her Manhattan at Chez Cody that evening. "I found his birth certificate online in the records of Allegheny County, Pennsylvania, which includes Pittsburgh. Nancy Upton Melonic was his mother's name; no father listed. Upton was probably *her* mother's maiden name, but I didn't check that. I did find a very sad obit for Nancy, who died at the age of thirty. Buck would have been three then. I'm assuming he wasn't adopted, since he kept the Melonic name. Maybe he went into foster care."

"How did she die?"

"The obit didn't say, but memorials were requested to something called the Allegheny Arts Alliance and to a sobriety house. I'm guessing she essentially died of acute alcoholism."

And her son was about three at the time. Our boys would be four the following month. I could hear them playing in the basement.

"You don't like Melonic much, do you?" Lynda said.

"No. I find him annoying. I think he has what Seth's new co-worker would call a melonic ego. Plus, he's cutting in on Seth."

"Well, cut him a break; he hasn't had an easy life. And working out of the West Virginia bureau of America's smallest news service doesn't indicate that he's setting the world on fire as a journalist. He probably thinks his reporting on this case will get him a leg up on a better job."

"That reminds me." I told her what Seth said about the upcoming announcement at the *Observer.*

Lynda frowned. "That can't be good. Johanna didn't tell me."

"Maybe she doesn't want you to worry. It does sound ominous. What did you find out about Gamaliel Taylor?"

"Well, he wasn't lying when he said he visited Erin years ago. It was in 1978. Fortunately, back issues of the *Observer* have been digitized going back to 1970. There was a two-day art fair that he was part of, but he seems to have been around a little longer. He gave a lecture at the Shinkle called, 'Art Is Always Modern,' and his name shows up a few times in the 'Around the Town' column that used to appear before Fred Gaffe started 'The Old Gaffer.' Taylor must have parked the predecessor to his Airstream here for a while."

Lynda sipped her cocktail. She was enjoying this.

"And why were we looking at him?" I asked. "Oh, yeah, because he's not from this area and may not have realized that violets are all over the place and he didn't have to buy the African variety." That suddenly seemed weak, although it was my idea before it was Lynda's idea. "Remind me what motive he might have?"

She wrinkled her eyebrows in thought. "Um, maybe Des was the real target all along?"

"Because?"

"She could have been *enceinte,* as Mac might say—not impossible at age 42; it happened to my grandmother—and he didn't like the idea of changing diapers."

That would have been a good motive in 1956.

I picked up my phone. "I'd better let poor Seth know what you found out about Melonic. And Mac, too." I texted both of them.

"The end of this case is just around the corner," I assured Popcorn the next morning.

Unfortunately, that corner is nowhere around here—maybe Fifth and Madison in New York.

She looked skeptical.

After a few hours of companionable working with her and Riley St. Simon, our magenta-haired intern, I made the trek to Mac's office. Amazingly, he was behind the screen of his computer and not practicing card tricks or making coins disappear.

"Ah, Jefferson! To what do I owe the pleasure?"

"I needed a new place to mope. Too bad the Melonic name thing didn't work out."

"Ah, well, 'What's in a name?' after all."

"Right. This case is full of the same name—Bainbridge. Mostly prefaced by a moniker stolen from Shakespeare—Ophelia, Portia, Desdemona, even Juliet. And you said the flowers came from Shakespeare, too."

He nodded, the McCabe brain clearly engaged. "Not just from Shakespeare. I have the unshakeable feeling that those flowers are together in the same passage. By thunder, Monica will know!"

And before I knew it, we were engaged in a Facebook Messenger call with Monica Porlock, Ph.D., author of *A Rose by Any Other Name: The Language of Flowers in Shakespeare*. She was a handsome older woman in the elegant Saylor-Mackie mode, with black hair attractively streaked with gray.

"Sebastian McCabe!" she gushed. "What a nice surprise! It's been ages. To what do I owe the pleasure?"

Gag me with a ladle!

"Too long indeed. Time's winged chariot, and all that. This is my brother-in-law and friend, Thomas Jefferson Cody. We were hoping you could identify a passage from the Bard that mentions three specific flowers."

"A single passage?"

"I believe so. The flowers are columbine, rosemary, and violets."

"Do they have to be in that order?" Porlock asked.

"That is unknown."

"Well, there's a famous passage where all of those flowers appear, along with a lot of others. It's from *Hamlet*, Act Four, Scene Five. I think I quoted from it in *A Rose by Any Other Name*."

I can't say whether Mac turned red behind his beard. "Hell and damnation! You did indeed, Monica. I read that passage when I looked up columbines in the index of the book after Ophelia's demise. And then I promptly forgot it."

Porlock didn't. She gave it to him from memory:

"'There's rosemary, that's for remembrance:
pray you, love, remember: and there is pansies,
that's for thoughts.
There's fennel for you, and columbines:
there's rue for you; and here's some for me:
we may call it herb of grace o' Sundays: O
you must wear your rue with a difference.
There's a daisy: I would give you some violets,
but they withered when my father died:'"

"And that means what, exactly?" I inquired. I was at sea as much as I was the first time I heard it.

"This is Ophelia talking at the end of a famous scene where she passes out flowers, all of which have meaning," Porlock said. "She's been driven mad by the fact that she loves Hamlet, who not only spurns her but kills her father."

Macbeth is cheerier.

"I recall now that in the book you said that columbine here may mean folly or foolishness, flattery or insincerity, or fortitude," Mac reminded her.

She looked surprised. "Did I? Well, that was thirty years ago in my callow youth. It was my first book, which was my doctoral dissertation. After more mature reflection, I would say today that columbine in this context stands for insincerity. And then, more obviously, rosemary stands for remembrance and violets for faithlessness—the opposite of the usual meaning—because they are withered."

"Taken together, then, that floral trio might indicate a memory of someone's insincerity and faithlessness," Mac said, stroking his hairy phiz.

"In the context of *Hamlet*, yes. But, of course, each of those flowers has other meanings as well. The columbines could stand for love, another ancient meaning, and the violets would be for faithfulness if they weren't withered."

Mac's eyebrows reached for the sky. "By thunder, yes! Perhaps the shriveling of the violets was unintended."

"What are you babbling about?" Porlock demanded. "What's going on?"

"We are investigating the tragic slayings of three women, triplets, one of whom was a colleague of mine on the

St. Benignus faculty. Their father, Ezra Bainbridge, asked me to look into it."

"I saw something about the murders on PNN, but it never occurred to me that Ezra is their father." She shook her head. "I know him from the American Shakespeare Association." *Of course! If there are Sherlockian societies by the score, why not Shakespearean ones, or at least one?* "He's neither an academic nor a theatrical person, but he's been generous to libraries, museums, and so forth in connection with various Shakespearean pursuits."

Mac nodded. "That is quite in character for him. At St. Benignus—" He stopped. "Ezra! Of course! You really have been most helpful, Monica! I owe you."

"Buy me a drink at the next Modern Language Association meeting and tell me how this came out."

"My guess is you'll see it on PNN," I told her.

Mac disconnected.

"What about Ezra?" I asked Mac.

"Grady Sanders was right, old boy." It took me a second to remember the manager at The Bull's Eye. "He said the most important thing the Bainbridge sisters had in common was their father and mother. Mr. Melonic was ludicrously off-base in suggesting that Ophelia—because of the Shakespearean implications of the flowers—could have been a suspect if not a victim. Ophelia studied and wrote about twentieth century American fiction and poetry. She was no Shakespearean

"But her father is."

Chapter Twenty-Seven
The Evil That Men Do

"GK isn't going to like this," I said, thinking about seeing "St. Benignus University trustee" after Ezra's name in a news story.

"Nor do I, Jefferson, I assure you," Mac riposted.

It took a few hours to pull it all together, but by early afternoon we were back at Ezra's library along with the surviving Bainbridges, David Gunner, Gamaliel Taylor, Lucius Snedeker, Tall Rawls, and Buck Melonic. Oscar was missing because Mac was hoping to get a confession before looping him in, but that turned out to be a good thing.

It wasn't easy to get the lady and gentleman of the press in the house, but Mac gave Fleur a song and dance about how accurate reporting could do no one any harm. I think he just wanted to show off. No matter his reason, he had only himself to blame for what happened in front of the journalists.

"Are you sure you want to have an audience for this?" I asked while he was rounding up his guest list. Full marks to me for that. "You're rowing out into some pretty deep water without a life preserver." *Not bad!* I made a mental note to use that one again. No doubt I'll have the opportunity.

"I am sure of nothing," Mac said grimly. *That's a first.* "But the Shakespearean flowers, the killer's easy entrance into the three homes, the violence of the murders, and the sheer madness of it all adds up. These were murders for love—Ezra Bainbridge's love for his Juliet."

Eyeballing Ezra a few hours later sitting in his wheelchair, looking lost, it was hard to buy that he was behind it all. He looked about a hundred years old, a once-vigorous man collapsed in on himself. But you know what they say about appearances. And maybe the whole long COVID thing was a dodge, or maybe it only affected his mind in some weird way and he pretended to be frailer than he was.

Mac stood in the middle of the impressive library and looked around at Ezra Bainbridge and his remaining family. "On the theory that it is better to inflict pain swiftly than to do so slowly, I will be direct," Mac said. "Ezra, I believe that you have for forty-two years harbored bitter feelings against your three daughters because they were the instrument of your wife's death when she passed away during childbirth."

"What?" It was an expression of disbelief, not failure to understand. Mac's assertion had pierced the brain fog. "That's ridiculous," Ezra mumbled. "I loved my girls. My little girls. 'Good morning to you, fair and gracious daughter.'"[17] Tears started running down both cheeks.

"How dare you, McCabe!" Fleur exploded. She knelt next to her husband and took his hand.

"What the hell!" Goldie said at the same time. She said a few other things too. David Gunner held *her* hand.

"This is as painful for me as it is for you," Mac said. If anybody else had said that he would have called out the cliché. "The murderer was sending the world a message about his feelings for his late wife through the flowers left with the

---

[17] *Measure for Measure*, Act IV, Scene 3—*S. McCabe.*

bodies of the three women who killed her by their birth— rosemary for remembrance, columbine for love, violets for faithfulness. In doing so, he drew from a passage of his beloved Shakespeare, although intending alternative meanings for the flowers than those in that text.

"Any other killer might have simply grabbed violets out of someone's lawn, given that there are none in the English garden at Stratford Court. For Ezra, who is not easily mobile, that was not feasible. So he bought violets, most likely by mail order. And yet, do not forget, Ezra is not completely immobile. He can walk with the aid of a cane—I have seen him do so—and he could have walked, albeit with difficulty, to each of his daughters' homes, where he would be welcomed without question."

"No," Ezra muttered.

"This is insane," Gunner informed us.

"So was King Lear," Melonic said. "And he had three daughters." That took me back: Ezra had made the same observation to Mac and me the day we visited with him in his library at the beginning of this mess; or, rather, the beginning of our involvement.

"You bastard!" Gamaliel Taylor yelled, but not at Mac. He was addressing the old man in the wheelchair. "You knew you weren't their father. That's why you killed them."

Stunned silence filled the room to overflowing for maybe ten seconds, which is longer than you think, then all hell broke loose with exclamations of incredulity and/or surprise. As for Sebastian McCabe, he kept his mouth shut. Maybe he figured he'd said enough already. Or maybe he just didn't know what to say. He looked like a man who'd had a horse shot out from under him.

"I think you need to explain," Gunner told Taylor when the room quieted down.

"Yes, I suppose I had better," the artist said. "I have from time to time alluded to the fact that I visited this godforsaken town decades ago. At that time, I became intimate with Juliet Bainbridge, one of a great number of women whose delights I have looked back on with great fondness in these later years. I have long suspected that I was the father of her daughters, who were born the appropriate number of months after I departed. In recent years I have followed them long-distance through the internet."

"Holy shit!" Lucius Snedeker said, taking the words right out of my mind.

I mentally thwacked myself in the head. Lynda's research into the *Observer* archives showed that Taylor was in Erin in 1978, the year before the tripletswere born. I should have done the math. Or maybe biology was the science that should have clued me in: The Bainbridge women were all tall and fair, like Taylor and unlike their medium-sized father and their auburn-haired mother. That sort of thing does tend to run in families; Kate and I are both tall redheads. And who was it who observed that Taylor was old enough to be Des's father? Oh, yeah. Portia.

"When I determined to meet these three offspring, it was no great difficulty to strike up an acquaintance with the most artistic and make it appear to be happenstance. Then the Shinkle artist-in-residence program made a wonderful excuse to present myself in Erin."

Melonic stared at him. "That's some yarn, and I'm not sure I buy it. Your daughters, if they are your daughters, are forty-two years old. What made you suddenly decide to take a fatherly interest?"

"Pancreatic cancer, as Samuel Johnson said about hanging in a fortnight, concentrates the mind wonderfully. My doctor assures me that I have no need to be concerned about next year's mid-term election." That accounted for Taylor's weight loss I'd noticed at the garden party and again in his Airstream. "It seemed time for me to get to know some of the wild oats I sowed in younger years. I'd planned to reveal my parentage to Des, Portia, and Ophelia, but I couldn't work myself up to it in time." He addressed Ezra: "You robbed me of that, you sterile old cuckold."

Ezra, staring straight ahead, said nothing.

"I should have known," Mac muttered. "Context is everything. The rosemary, columbine, and withered violets on the bodies meant just what they meant in *Hamlet*: A memory of Juliet's insincerity and faithlessness. That's what the existence of your three daughters meant to you, Ezra. That provides a very different motive from what I posited a few moments ago, but an equally strong one."

The old man shook his head while Fleur stared daggers at Mac.

"Why would Grandpa hurt Mom and my aunts after all this time?" Goldie said.

"Perhaps he just found out," Mac said. He turned to Taylor. "Did you tell him?"

"No. Why would I?"

"I've always known." Ezra spoke through barely moving lips. He looked over at Fleur, still kneeling beside him. "Bring me *Shakespeare the Catholic* by Margaret Lewis. Third shelf from the top, fourth book from the left."

She used a stepstool to reach it.

Ezra took the book from her with trembling hands and opened it up. Just inside the front cover was a cream-colored envelope with an 8-cent LOVE postage stamp canceled on November 8, 1978. He opened that and pulled out two sheets of paper in the same color, covered with writing in a feminine hand. "This is the letter Juliet wrote to me when she found out she was pregnant. I was in England the month that Taylor was here. She confessed everything and asked my forgiveness. She mailed it to me from a girlfriend's house in Savannah to give me time." His eyes glistened. "It took me two days to write her back, but when I did, I told her to come home. I loved her. I loved the girls because she was part of them. The other part didn't matter."

I would have bet my Roth IRA that this was all new to Fleur, but she didn't express the slightest surprise. What a trouper! "Satisfied now?" she asked Mac.

"Would that I were!" And I'm sure he meant it. "Granted that Ezra knew all these years that Juliet's daughters were not his own, it could be that Mr. Taylor's return to Erin resurfaced some long-buried emotions, exacerbated by the mental effects of long COVID."

"This has gone on long enough," Gunner said.

"It certainly has," Fleur agreed. "I wanted to hear what you had to say," she told Mac, "but I've heard enough. The longer we stay, the more theories you'll come up with to justify your conclusion." She picked up one of her husband's trembling hands and let it fall. "Parkinson's. There's no strength in these hands. Ezra could barely open that book. And he certainly couldn't bludgeon anyone to death."

Challenge to the Reader

The worst part of that whole sorry episode in Ezra's library was that Mac had everything he needed to solve three murders and thereby (spoiler alert!) prevent a fourth murder. But he didn't see it. Neither did anybody else. Do you? You have all the facts that Mac and I had at this point. Who killed the Bainbridge triplets?

Chapter Twenty-Eight
There's Rue for You

"I should have suspected Gamaliel Taylor's paternity," Mac said as he exceeded the speed limit leaving Stratford Court behind us. "His revulsion at the suggestion of a sexual relationship with Desdemona when we interviewed him in his Airstream was simultaneously out of character and quite genuine. There had to be a unique reason he called the notion 'a bridge too far' and was so offended."

This struck me as somewhat akin to the builder of a caved-in building saying he'd made an error in his choice of windows, but I was smart enough not to say so. Sarcasm may be my superpower, but I know when not to use it. Seldom, if ever, had I seen Sebastian McCabe fire with blanks in such a public setting. True, Tall Rawls and Buck Melonic wrote nary a word of what happened, but that didn't do much to soothe the McCabe ego. Everyone in Ezra's library that day knew, and word filtered up to the SBU's president's office.

"What the hell does McCabe think he's doing?" GK thundered to me in a phone call the next day.

Am I my brother-in-law's keeper?

"At the moment I'm pretty sure he's trying to fly below the radar," I said.

"You know what I mean! The next time he accuses one of my trustees of murder, tell him not to do it. Especially if the trustee is innocent!"

He hung up before I could defend myself and Mac, in that order. And if you're wondering why I got the call instead of the object of GK's ire, I can only say this wasn't the first time I took one for the team.

Mac went around in a blue funk for the next three days, short-tempered and growling. I had that from Lynda, who had it from Kate. Oscar must have been equally good company, judging from Popcorn's mood. But I didn't ask.

And then, on Friday evening shortly after I got home from work ready to unwind for the weekend, my phone rang.

"Uh-oh," I told Lynda. "It's Mac."

"There goes cocktail hour, darling."

She was right, of course. This wasn't a social call.

"Marigold Bainbridge found the body of Gamaliel Taylor earlier today at his travel camper," Mac reported. He sounded like his old buoyant self.

"Well, that was fast. I had the impression his sell-by date was a little further out."

"It was a blow to the head that took his life, not cancer."

"Murder? But he was a dead man walking. He implied that he didn't have much more than a year to live."

"Intriguing, is it not?" Mac said. "Our presence has been requested at the scene of the murder."

"I'd think the Bainbridges would wear garlic to keep us away."

"It was Oscar who called me."

"Is he that desperate?"

"Indeed, old boy. His officers have followed every clue to no avail, the pressure from the prosecutor has not diminished with each passing day, and now he faces yet a fourth murder. Still, I gather Oscar made the decision to seek our assistance only reluctantly. The coroner has come and gone, giving her immediate opinion that Mr. Taylor has been dead some time, certainly more than a day."

We arrived at the scene to find Goldie Bainbridge standing outside the Airstream with her father, Lucius Snedeker. I thought, *What, no David Gunner?*

"I repeat," Goldie told Oscar just as we decamped Mac's car, "I want to go home. You have no grounds for holding me here. I'm supposed to be having dinner with David."

"I'm not holding you, Ms. Bainbridge," the Chief said. He looked about five years older than the last time I saw him. "I just want you to tell Mac what happened."

"That bungler!"

She pointedly didn't look at said bungler, although she must have seen him coming. He's hard to miss.

Her father put her arm around her. "The path of least resistance, sweetheart—just take it! That's how I survive. Just do what the Chief asks and get on with your life."

"I would appreciate it," Mac rumbled.

She gave a theatrical sigh. "Over the last couple of days, I noticed that a few of my mother's things were missing—some jewelry, a photo of her and Dad when they were expecting me, a couple of her paintings that I liked, things like that. I started to suspect that maybe Gamaliel took them as mementos. I still can't believe that man was my grandfather!"

"Believe it," Mac said.

"Yeah, well, anyway. I called him for two days and didn't get any answer, so I decided on a frontal assault. Dad said he'd go with me. We got here and pounded on the door. No answer. Well, I thought maybe he was just avoiding us, so I tried the door. It was unlocked. Like characters in some stupid movie, we walked in and there he was." Her voice quivered. Apparently finding the second body was no easier than the first, even though they hadn't been close.

"And he'd been bashed from behind?" I asked. I guess I could have been more tactful.

"He was struck with a bottle of 12-year-old single malt scotch called The Dalmore," Oscar reported.

Mac raised an eyebrow. "Not an expensive piece of artwork?"

"He didn't have any."

"And there were flowers scattered on or near the body?" Mac asked.

Oscar had no time for obvious questions. "Of course, there were blankety-blank flowers!" He didn't actually say "blankety-blank."

"*Ruta graveolens,*" Snedeker said. "We have some in the garden, although it's not English. It's native to the Balkan peninsula. It's an herb, really, a bitter one, sometimes called herb-of-grace, but more commonly—"

"Rue," Mac said. "As in 'there's rue for you.'"

"What?" Oscar demanded.

"A quote from Shakespeare," I informed him. "He was a writer."

The next morning, I began my weekend by noodling over all this with Mac in the man cave of his sprawling home at 23 Half Moon Street. Because it's where he writes his mystery novels, he's under the illusion it's an office. But I call a room with a fireplace, comfortable chairs, beer taps, and even a fountain of Caffeine-Free Diet Coke for me, a man cave. I also call it cool.

"Well, at least we know what Taylor had in common with the other three victims," I said.

Mac glowered. "And Ezra had even more reason to kill him. Except that it was physically impossible, not to mention the unlikelihood that Mr. Taylor would have welcomed him into his abode."

"Still, Taylor's connection to his daughters can't be a coincidence. Maybe he should have kept a lower profile about his paternity."

Kate stuck her head in the door. "I don't think it was in that man's DNA to keep a lower profile. Narcissists don't do that."

"What?" Mac looked startled at first, then his face lit up like a kid on Christmas morning. "DNA!" he bellowed.

"What about it?" Kate wanted to know.

"Myrtle White mentioned in passing that Ophelia took a DNA test."

I dimly recalled that. "Are you thinking that she knew Taylor was her father?"

"No, old boy, I am thinking along entirely different lines. I am sure you noticed that the Bainbridge sisters were tall and fair like their true biological father and unlike Ezra."

"You aren't sure of that at all, but I actually did."

"Bravo! Those four are not the only individuals in this case who share those characteristics, however. I believe I know the identity of the killer."

"You believed that before," Kate reminded Mac.

Ouch.

"And I shall redeem myself from that painful fiasco to which you allude with a call to the media."

"Are you sure you want to do that?" I said.

Without answering that very sensible question, Mac surprised me by calling Buck Melonic first.

"I am ready to unveil the murderer," he announced.

"Again?" came the voice on a speakerphone.

Mac ignored the sarcasm. "Where are you?"

"We're on our way to the graveside service for Desdemona Bainbridge at St. Saviour's Cemetery. The funeral just ended."

"You speak in the plural. Is Johanna with you, by any chance?"

"Hi, Mac!" came her familiar voice.

"We will meet you at the cemetery," Mac said, and quickly disconnected.

His next call was to Oscar, telling me he needed backup this time.

We saw the Stinson & Company hearse unloading as we pulled into the spacious graveyard. Seeing the remaining Bainbridges (Fleur behind her husband's wheelchair), one ex-husband, one ex-paramour, and one current boyfriend/lawyer, all I could think was "Round up the usual suspects!"

They were all looking our way as we pulled up in Mac's mammoth vehicle, and none of them happily. They all looked like undertakers, even the undertakers (presumably Mr. Stinson and Mr. Company).

"You're not welcome here, Professor McCabe," Goldie informed him when we got within hailing range. "I thought you would have the decency to understand that. It's bad enough to have the media vultures here."

Johanna colored. Melonic seemed unconcerned.

Mac gave a slight bow. "I do understand, Miss Bainbridge, and I beg your indulgence. I have something to say, and I will keep it as brief as I can. However, I do think Chief Hummel will wish to hear it."

Oscar was ambling our way and soon arrived. He tipped his official hat at the bereaved. "Sorry to intrude." He flashed Mac a *"you'd better be right"* look.

"Let's get this over with," Fleur said.

"Very well," Mac said. "First, I apologize again for my mistaken suspicion of Ezra." The old man looked up as if that name sounded vaguely familiar. "I was horribly wrong. I was wrong about almost everything in this case, except at the very beginning. I was mistaken in thinking early on that I was mistaken."

Got that?

David Gunner opened his mouth, but Mac moved on quickly.

"When the body of my friend and colleague Ophelia Bainbridge was found with several columbine flowers, I immediately assumed that she was trying to leave a dying message—just like the victim in so many of the Ellery Queen stories that she loved. And I was correct. The flowers at the other murders were red herrings, left by the killer to distort the meaning of Ophelia's message and to falsely point to Ezra."

I knew where this was going, so I kept my eye on said killer as Mac laid it out.

"Ophelia was a woman who loved all manner of wordplay. She especially enjoyed anagrams. You will recall that the rather unusual pseudonym of Lia Hope Gabbierdin under which she wrote her mystery reviews was an anagram of Ophelia Bainbridge. In a similar way, the flower that she left was an anagram of her killer's name."

"That's absurd!" Arlo said. "You're telling us she thought of an anagram as she was dying?"

"By no means! She must have noticed the anagram earlier. In her mind, then, she associated the columbine with his name. That is why she grabbed the flower as a clue after the killer departed. And when that killer learned about the columbine found in close proximity to her body, he understood the meaning. Fortunately for him, that was far from obvious to anyone else. He could not be sure that would continue to be the case, however. So he added flowers to the bodies of her sisters, whose murders he planned from the beginning, so that we would cease believing that Ophelia had left a dying message and would assume—as we did—that it was the killer who was making a statement.

"To give the devil his due, if he had not done that I may have realized much sooner that the word 'columbine' is an anagram for B.U. Melonic."

Chapter Twenty-Nine
Truth Will Out

Melonic looked at the faces around him, maybe trying to get a read on whether they were buying it. Or maybe he was calculating the odds of making a run for it. But given that Gibbons and Lehmann had just pulled up in a patrol car, escape was a non-starter.

The reporter gave a laugh that wouldn't have passed muster with the director of a fifth-grade play. "You're kidding. I may be a lousy amateur sleuth, but even I could come up with something better than that."

Johanna's Nordic face—not hard-stopping gorgeous like Lynda, but pretty and sweet—told me that she wanted to believe her suitor but couldn't quite wrap her mind around the idea that Mac would make another blunder in this case.

"What possible reason could Buck have for killing anybody in Erin?" she objected. "He didn't even know them."

"Yes, he did," Gunner said. "You're forgetting that he interviewed Ophelia for a feature story. He reminded me of that when he tried to get into Ezra's house."

"And Ophelia had taken a DNA test, presumably through one of the many commercial companies that make that service available," Mac said. "She mentioned that to her colorist, Myrtle White, and Myrtle mentioned it to us."

"So?" Oscar said. "That's trending. Lots of people take DNA tests."

"Precisely! And I am convinced that one of them was B.U. Melonic."

"Buck's the name," Melonic snapped.

Tall Rawls wasn't missing a word of this. Neither was her notebook.

Mac ploughed on: "No one awake to the reality of human frailty could be entirely surprised to find out that Gamaliel Taylor was the real father of the Bainbridge triplets once we had been told. He, like they, was tall and fair. So is Mr. Melonic. Such similarities are not unusual in families. Undoubtedly, Mr. Melonic took a DNA test and found out that he was the brother of someone else who had done likewise—Ophelia Bainbridge."

"And he didn't know that Taylor was his father?" Snedeker asked.

Mac shook his head. "His father's name was not on his birth certificate. Nor, presumably, was Mr. Taylor in the DNA database. Nancy Upton Melonic, his mother, was unwed. We know that from some research Lynda Cody undertook to determine whether Mr. Melonic's name was genuine. Miss Melonic's obituary asked that memorials be sent to the Allegheny Arts Alliance. Was she an artist, Mr. Melonic, like Juliet Bainbridge?"

"She took a few drawing classes," he mumbled. "What if Taylor was my father? What does that prove?"

Mac didn't answer directly.

"When you researched the Bainbridge family after your DNA test results—easy for anyone to do in this internet age, and much more so for a trained reporter such as yourself—you had every reason to assume that the wealthy

Ezra Bainbridge was the triplets' father, and your own father
as well. The difference was that while they were raised in
wealth and comfort, you grew up in penury. It grated on you
that biology is not destiny, although I would argue that in
many respects that is a very good thing."

I looked at Ezra and had to look away.

"What must have seemed to you a grave injustice
undoubtedly rankled, and festered," Mac was saying. "A
demon named revenge entered your heart. You decided to
take away from Ezra Bainbridge what is most precious to any
parent —his children. And you would do so one by one, and
then frame Ezra for the murder. In each case the victim
allowed you to enter the house, fearing nothing from a
reporter. You had called first on a burner phone to make sure
she was alone. And then you struck her in the back of the
head with an expensive piece of artwork. That should have
been a psychological clue. Was it on purpose that you killed
with what must have seemed to you an extravagance?"

Melonic, lighting his pipe, chose not to answer.

"I suspect that it was, given that you asked Chief
Hummel at the news conference whether he saw significance
in the murder weapons all being relatively expensive pieces
of artwork."

Oscar glowered at Melonic.

"There were any number of clues that I recognized
only in retrospect," Mac told the rest of us. "For example,
Mr. Melonic said he conceived the idea of his story about
Ophelia from reading Hadley Reams's feature story about her
in *The Erin Observer & News-Ledger*. Why would a wire service
reporter in Wheeling be reading the *Observer*? Undoubtedly,

he saw the story when he was conducting an internet search of her name after learning that she was his sister."

"But wouldn't Ophelia know from the DNA report that Melonic was her brother?" Arlo objected. "And wouldn't she tell her sisters that they had an unknown sibling?"

"Those are good questions to which I believe I can surmise the answers. They are as follows: Mr. Melonic took the DNA test under another name. And Ophelia probably had been quietly attempting to find this non-existent person and learn his story before alerting her sisters to the startling news. Have you any response to that, Mr. Melonic?"

"No."

"I thought not. At any rate, Ophelia told me that while interviewing her Mr. Melonic asked enough questions to write a biography. Very likely that is when he learned the extent of the Bainbridge wealth that allowed his three half-sisters to live in such more-than-comfortable circumstances. And that knowledge ate away at him like a cancer until he resolved on his plan of revenge. He returned to Erin and killed Ophelia Bainbridge. I should have known when he turned up as a reporter the day after the murder that he scarcely had time to learn about the killing that morning, drive the four hours from Wheeling to Erin, interview Ezra Bainbridge, and stop at Portia and Arlo Bainbridge's house before encountering us at the *Observer* offices immediately after lunch. I have not covered myself with glory in this case."

"You apparently have a gift for understatement," Fleur told him. Mac continued:

"I suspect that Mr. Melonic's editor at the Central News Service will confirm for us that he was not assigned to the Bainbridge murders, at least not the first one."

"So?" Melonic said. He blew pipe smoke in Mac's direction. "Journalistic initiative is rewarded at CNS."

"Ah, yes, the reporter at work! Your role as a journalist allowed you to stay close to the investigation." *And to Johanna!* "So you learned early on about the dying message Ophelia left. She had probably mentioned to you that 'columbine' is an anagram of your byline name, which is how you understood the significance of her message. And you were afraid that in good time I or the police would discover it as well. Ironically, Jefferson did pay some attention to the name Melonic, but only on the errant premise that it might have been a false name. At any rate, you decided to give those flowers another meaning, one that would eventually point to Ezra as the killer—a deranged murderer indicating his motive through the language of flowers in Shakespeare."

"Shakespeare," Ezra said, a smile on his vacant face.

"You drew your inspiration from a book on that subject in Ezra's library," Mac told Melonic, "an electronic copy of which, by your own account, you downloaded. You even called my attention to it after Portia's murder. You were constantly probing my thoughts on the one hand and trying to implant your own on the other."

"You told *me* about that book after Ophelia's murder!" Melonic said.

"To my eternal regret! And you fed that back to me so that I would be sure not to miss your manufactured clues. I suspect, however, that you never actually read the book. Most likely you searched the index for 'columbine,' just as I did, and found the same passage from Hamlet that supplied all the flowers you used later. We should have paid more attention to the fact that, as an outsider, you were one of a small group of people in this case who would have gone to the trouble of securing an African violet when you could have plucked the more common variety out of the earth."

At one point that had seemed to point to Gamaliel Taylor. Right church, wrong pew.

"You suggested that because of the flower clues and their possible connection to Shakespeare, Ophelia would be a suspect if she were alive. I should have realized that rang false. You knew that she wasn't a Shakespearean. That was clear in your feature story about her. Your only point in making that comment was to turn my thoughts toward Stratford-upon-Avon, thinking that would ultimately lead me to Ezra Bainbridge. As it did, to my shame.

"When I wrongly accused Ezra, the truth about the triplets' paternity and yours came out. You were shocked to find out by Gamaliel Taylor's declaration and Ezra's admission that Ezra was not the father you shared with your victims, Mr. Melonic. By this point there was no subtlety left in you. Gamaliel Taylor had to die for abandoning your mother, and quickly, by the means at hand—no expensive artwork this time. The rue left at the scene was just to complete the pattern. There was no real attempt to frame Ezra; there was no longer any desire to. You may have even felt sorry for him if that is within your emotional repertoire."

And then Mac stopped talking.

"Is that it?" Melonic asked. "You're finished?"

"I am."

"Well," he said, looking around, "I must say that's quite a theory! But I didn't hear anything about proof."

"Ah, there's the rub," Mac said.

Chapter Thirty
All's Well That Ends Well

Gibbons got the proof, although it took him more than a week of physical and electronic searching. To wit:

(a) The burner phone used to call the victims and make sure they were alone before he came calling was hidden in the trunk of Melonic's car.

(b) Melonic stayed at a hotel in Licking Falls, about an hour from Erin, the day of Ophelia's murder, rather than driving in the next day after learning of the crime.

(c) License plate scanners from a private company (there are dozens in the industry, and they cooperate with law enforcement) confirmed that his red Honda FIT was in Erin on the murder day, and hours before he said he had been the following morning.

(d) Melonic's DNA, obtained under warrant, proved that he was related to the Bainbridge sisters, who were not related to Ezra Bainbridge.

So, Sebastian McCabe got it right in the end, but don't expect him to bring up the case. "Perhaps it was my last bow, old boy," he told me one moody afternoon in his man cave. I wouldn't bet on it, though.

Despite all that, Melonic is still pleading innocent. I don't know how Erica Slade, Erin's premier defender of the indicted, is going to play her hand—and her ex-husband, the prosecutor—but it should be entertaining. The trial starts in six weeks with Judge Irene Cassorla Kessler presiding.

Ezra Bainbridge is still an SBU trustee and supported GK's plan to reduce faculty and make tenure rarer. He's bouncing back physically from COVID under the loving attention of his wife, with a lot of help from Goldie. But he will never be the same man.

"I wasn't really all that smitten with Buck," Tall Rawls assured Lynda and me a couple of weeks ago at dinner while Seth Miller was in the little boys' room. "It was just business. Still, he is tall. Buck, I mean."

Seth hasn't asked me for any romantic advice lately, which I take as a good sign.

Johanna's job seems secure for a while under the new ownership of *The Erin Observer & News Ledger*. Serena Mason, my favorite multimillionaire, bought the paper! That's what she was in the office to talk to Frank Woodford about that day. She was negotiating her way up the food chain at Grier Media, but she wanted Frank to be in the loop. Serena asked Lynda to be the editor and publisher, but she turned it down.

"I was very flattered, darling," my spouse told me, "but I enjoy being a stay-at-home novelist. At least for now."

Serena didn't want to give the title to anyone else, so she kept it for herself. Ben Silverstein will continue to run the journalism side of the operation, but with more money to do it because Serena isn't out to make a profit. Frank Woodford is happy as a pig in mud being "editor at large," which means he gets to glad-hand in the community as before plus write a column called "To Be Frank." No more jobs to cut and budgets to balance!

Although the buck stops at Serena's desk, she'll have help at the 30,000-foot-level from a community board of directors representing finance (Amy Quong, executive vice president of Gamble Bank), business (Bobbie McGee), academia (the redoubtable Lesley Saylor-Mackie), the arts (Rosalie Gamble Hawthorne), and even journalism (former TV anchorwoman Nadine Lattimore). I see a certain pattern there, and it's a good one.

The leaves are falling now as I write, and Lynda and I took the kids for a walk at St. Saviour's Cemetery the other day.

"I still can't believe the man killed his own siblings," Lynda said.

"That started with Cain and Abel," I reminded her. "Hey, look who it is."

Goldie Bainbridge and David Gunner stood in front of her mother's headstone, holding hands. I noticed an engagement ring on Goldie's left finger. They saw us and waved. We caught up to them, introduced Donata and the boys, and said all the things one says at a gravesite. Then we drifted away, leaving a lot more unsaid.

This story began in a garden, and I will end it in a cemetery. But the theologically astute Sebastian McCabe assures me that a cemetery is a kind of garden, too.

A Few Words of Thanks

First, Jeff Cody and I would like to thank Mr. William Shakespeare for providing all the chapter titles for this eleventh novel and lucky thirteenth volume overall in the McCabe-Cody chronicles.

Even more important, however, are the members of Team Cody who so selflessly made this book possible:

Ann Brauer Andriacco, for roughing in the Stratford Court map finished by Brian Belanger, and for she-knows-what;

Jeff Suess, for proofreading; and

Steve Winter, yet again, for giving the manuscript the incredible benefit of his engineering eye.

Any errors that remain are mine, not theirs.

Publisher Steve Emecz and illustrator Brian Belanger are the easiest collaborators any writer was ever so lucky to have. MX Publishing is a social enterprise venture that is both enterprising and venturesome.

About the Author

Dan Andriacco has been reading mysteries since he discovered Sherlock Holmes at the age of about nine and writing them almost as long. His first published work, however, was a Sherlock Holmes pastiche short story in 1990. The McCabe-Cody series began in 2011.

After almost 24 years as a reporter and business editor of a daily newspaper, Dan served as communications director for a religious non-profit for 20 years. He holds a master's degree in religion and a doctorate in ministry.

A Baker Street Irregular ("St. Saviour's Near King's Cross"), Dan is the Most Scandalous Member (leader) of the Tankerville Club of Cincinnati and a member of numerous other scion societies of the BSI. He also wears bow ties. You can follow his long-running blog at www.danandriacco.com and his Facebook Fan Page, Dan Andriacco Mysteries.

Dan and his partner in criminous endeavors and in life, Ann Brauer Andriacco, have three grown children and six grandchildren. They live in Cincinnati, Ohio, USA, about forty miles downriver from the town of Erin, which is located on no map.

Also from MX Publishing

Visit www.mxpublishing.com for dozens of other Sherlock Holmes novels, novellas, short story collections, Conan Doyle biographies, Holmes travel books, and more.

MX Publishing is the award-winning, world's largest independent Sherlock Holmes Book publishers with over 150 new authors and 500 new Sherlock Holmes stories in print.

On Facebook:
https://www.facebook.com/BooksSherlockHolmes/

On Twitter
https://twitter.com/mxpublishing

On Instagram
https://www.instagram.com/mxpublishing/